SOARING EAGLE WOMAN

A MOUNTAIN MAN FRONTIER ADVENTURE

THE FRONTIER
BOOK 3

LEROY A. PETERS

ISBN: 9798333195852

❀ Created with Vellum

1

SURPRISE ATTACK

Fall of 1814
Yellowstone River
Near what is now Billings, Montana

IT WAS a quiet late September morning in the Crow village of Chief Medicine Hawk. About two days before, the village celebrated a successful buffalo hunt which had managed to secure enough meat and vegetables to prepared and ready them for the winter. Overlooking the village from a small cliff stood twenty-year-old trapper, Lazarus Buchanan. He first came out west from Delaware with his late uncle Amos MacKinnon four years ago. Amos was married to Medicine Hawk's daughter Plain Feather and they had a son named Angus White Cloud, who was now three years old. Amos was killed by a vengeful Blackfoot warrior named Lightning Strikes the previous year, however, Lazarus avenged his uncle's death.

For a while, Lazarus took care of his widowed aunt, until she remarried a Nez Perce warrior named Hawk Eyes this past summer.

Hawk Eyes was a good husband to Plain Feather and stepfather to Angus. Lazarus was happy for his aunt, that she had found someone new to love and protect her and her son. He knew that she never forgot his Uncle Amos and that he would not want her to mourn him for the rest of her life.

Lazarus had his own family to think about other than his aunt and cousin. For the past two years, the young trapper was the proud husband of not one but two wives—Dark Wind, who was Flathead and Mountain Flower who was Nez Perce, from Hawk Eyes' village. Dark Wind and Lazarus had a son themselves named Amos Winter Hawk. The little tyke would be two in January of next year, right after his father's birthday. Because of this, Lazarus was an adopted member of the Crow, Flathead, and Nez Perce tribes. Known as White Bear, which was a name first given to him by an Omaha War Chief named Yellow Bull, Lazarus had a well-deserved reputation as an honorable man who would fight to the death in order to protect his family and friends.

As he sat quietly on the cliff overlooking the village, Lazarus thought about his life over the past four years. He remembered being an impulsive sixteen-year-old who had just gotten kicked out of school for fighting, begging his uncle to take him back west with him to be a trapper and mountain man. After Amos promised Lazarus' parents and his own father that he would look out for the lad, he relented. It had been quite an adventure, thought Lazarus. After coming out west, Lazarus had met the legendary John Colter, who taught his Uncle Amos on how to be a trapper, he'd fought against hostile enemy tribes such as the Lakota and Blackfeet, fought and defeated rival trappers who were a threat to him and his family and friends. To top it all off, Lazarus had started a family of his own and formed alliances with the Omaha, Crow, Flathead, and Nez Perce.

Despite his fierce reputation, Lazarus didn't like killing. He did it only when he had to, and he had killed a lot of men both white and red who were a threat to him and his family and friends. Lazarus thought about his blood kin back east in Delaware. How would they react to him being the man he has become? How would his family treat his wives and son? At first, Lazarus pushed the thought from his mind. While he did miss his parents and siblings, he felt no reason to return to Delaware. The only blood relative that he loved and truly cared about was his Uncle Amos and he was no longer among the living. As if his Uncle's death wasn't enough, Lazarus, while visiting St. Louis this past summer, found out that the legendary mountain man John Colter had died from jaundice in November of last year. He'd became a friend to Lazarus thanks to his Uncle Amos. Both losses hit him hard, but Lazarus needed to keep going. His main focus now was his family and nothing or no one would keep him from protecting them at all costs.

As he stood up, grabbed his rifle, and was about to return to the village, he was pleasantly surprised to see his beloved wife Dark Wind standing before him.

"Are you alright husband?" she asked.

"Never better," answered Lazarus. He looked her up and down and was mesmerized. The couple had known each other for about four years, but had been married for two. Other than Mountain Flower, he considered her the most beautiful woman he had ever known and he let her know it. "Have I told you lately how beautiful you are?"

Dark Wind giggled. She loved it when he complimented her.

"I'm assuming our son is with Mountain Flower and Plain Feather."

"He is," answered Dark Wind.

"Well, we best get back to the village," he said.

Dark Wind approached and gently placed a hand on her husband's chest. "What's the hurry?"

Lazarus was grinning from ear to ear.

About an hour later the happy couple returned to the village. Both Angus White Cloud and Amos Winter Hawk were playing on a buffalo robe when Lazarus and Dark Wind entered the tipi. Plain Feather, Hawk Eyes, and Mountain Flower were all smiling at them when they came in.

"Took you long enough," said Plain Feather.

"We were occupied," laughed Lazarus. Both Plain Feather and her husband chuckled, as the baby boys ran to Lazarus. The big trapper picked up his son and cousin and tickled them as he sat down, before giving Mountain Flower a passionate kiss. "There will be more of that later," he said to her in Nez Perce.

"I am looking forward to it," she responded.

It was the middle of the afternoon, when a shout from the outskirts of the village was heard. Lazarus and Hawk Eyes grabbed their weapons and went to join the Crow warriors to investigate. The commotion was coming from the horse herd. Chief Medicine Hawk and his nephews Running Dog and Lame Deer were talking to some of the horse guards.

"What happened?" asked Lazarus.

"Little Otter says that he spotted a Lakota war party not far from here," answered Running Dog.

"We must get the women, children and elderly to safety," said Chief Medicine Hawk. Lame Deer and Lazarus, along with some warriors, volunteered to get the women, children, and elderly to safety, while the rest led by Chief Medicine Hawk went to meet their foes.

The Lakota tribe were longtime enemies of the Crow. They sojourned in what is now the states of North and South Dakota and Eastern Montana, but like most tribes of the Northern Plains, they were nomadic and followed the buffalo. While allies of the Cheyenne and Arapaho, the Lakota were enemies to the Arikara, Mandan, Hidatsa, Chippewa, Pawnee, Omaha, Flathead, Blackfeet, Shoshone, and Cree. The tribe consisted of seven bands: Brule, Oglala, San Arcs, Hunkpapa, Miniconjou, Blackfoot, and Two Kettles.

Chief Medicine Hawk led his Crow warriors to the outskirts of the village and put up a defensive perimeter. The oncoming Lakota paused about two hundred yards from the Crow defenders. The invaders were painted for war and were ready for a fight. The Lakota leader shouted his war cry and the invaders charged. What the Lakota didn't count on was that the Crow were not only armed with traditional bows and arrows, but also had rifles and muskets traded to them mostly with trappers like Lazarus Buchanan, who often supplied this village with rifles.

As the enemy charged, Chief Medicine Hawk fired his Kentucky rifle, a gift from Lazarus' Uncle Amos, hitting one Lakota warrior. The rest of the defenders followed suit with guns and bows and arrows, before charging at their hated enemy. The battle was fierce and personal. Some of the invaders made it through and managed to enter the village. However, the women, children, and elderly had made it out already and the Lakota invaders were greeted with fierce fire from some of the Crow defenders and their allies who'd stayed hidden in the village.

Lazarus managed to take down a Lakota warrior with his Pennsylvania rifle before another warrior attempted to charge at him. Lazarus took him down with one of his pistols, shooting him point blank in the head. Another invader who witnessed this attempted to charge at Lazarus on his horse, screaming his war cry. However, Lazarus took out his other pistol and shot the enemy's horse right out from under him. The warrior had the wind knocked out of him, but he managed to regain his composure and turned his attention to Lazarus, his rage at losing a prized horse evident in his burning eyes.

With no time to reload, Lazarus took out his Crow tomahawk and Arkansas toothpick, pointing the latter at the enemy invader, issuing him a challenge. The Lakota warrior accepted and in a split second the two men were locked in hand-to-hand combat. Lazarus had height, weight, and strength to his advantage, while the smaller, shorter warrior had speed. The warrior attempted to strike at Lazarus' midsection, but the trapper blocked his knife with his tomahawk. Lazarus countered with his own knife strike and managed to slice the enemy warrior on his side. This gave the warrior pause for a second as he was now bleeding profusely from the wound.

However, his pride overrode his caution. He wanted to kill this white-haired, white man who lived and fought beside his enemy, so he charged again, knife in hand. Lazarus again blocked the strike with his tomahawk, but this time he managed to jam his Arkansas toothpick into the Lakota warrior's ribcage. The enemy fell to his knees and began singing his death song. Lazarus wasted no time as he buried the tomahawk into the man's skull, killing him instantly.

2

AFTERMATH

THE BATTLE LASTED NO MORE than twenty minutes. Despite the fierceness of it, only three Crow defenders lost their lives. No women, children, or elderly were hurt or captured. Today was a huge victory for the Crow village of Medicine Hawk as they repelled the Lakota invaders. With Running Dog leading the Crow defenders in chasing their enemies back to their own country, Chief Medicine Hawk and the rest of the village defenders assessed the damage. The three warriors who died defending their home were quickly mourned as their bodies were brought in to their grieving families. Other than that, most of the defenders suffered minor injuries. The bodies of the Lakota invaders who were killed were quickly scalped and mutilated by both the men and women of the village.

As expected, Lazarus reluctantly scalped the three Lakota warriors he'd killed and left their bodies to the women to be beaten and mutilated. While the village was returning to normal, Running Dog and the Crow defenders returned.

"The Lakota dogs are gone," he said. "With their tails tucked between their legs."

"This is good," said Chief Medicine Hawk.

"Don't you find it strange that the Lakota would raid us this late in the season?" asked Lazarus. The question gave Chief Medicine Hawk and those who sat on the council food for thought.

"That is a very good question," said Hawk Eyes in Crow. While the warrior was not Crow, he was accepted by the village and just as Lazarus, was adopted as one and had defended his adopted people fiercely from their enemy. "Usually enemies such as the Lakota and the Blackfeet would usually raid during the beginning of spring to the middle of summer," he said.

"This is true," responded Blue Willow, Chief Medicine Hawk's wife. As the bodies of the Lakota invaders who were killed were being beaten by the women, Chief Medicine Hawk and some of those who sat on the council momentarily stopped them so they could get a good look at the bodies.

"These warriors are not old men," he said. "Most of them don't look to be older than twenty summers."

"The one that I killed in hand-to-hand combat didn't look that much younger than me," said Lazarus. Some of the Crow defenders, including Running Dog and Lame Deer, were saying the same thing. Most of the Lakota warriors they battled against today appeared to be at the most in their early to mid-twenties.

"This explains a lot," said Plain Feather. "Young boys trying to prove they are men and warriors."

"I have seen such pride among our own men," added her mother.

Chief Medicine Hawk just smiled, but he, too, was a little sad. While he had no love for his enemies, he found no joy in knowing that Lakota mothers would never see their sons again or that young Lakota wives were now widows.

"Nothing kills a young man more than pride," he said.

"Sounds like something my grandfather would say," said Lazarus.

"A wise man, White Bear," said Chief Medicine Hawk. "Your Uncle was the same way. He believed that pride was lethal."

Meanwhile, the Lakota raiding party returned to their home near Bear Mountain. The raid against their Crow enemies was a disaster. Even worse, the leader of the raid, River Fox, was killed in battle. His friend Broken Arrow witnessed his death at the hands of a white-haired, white man, who was living among and fighting with the Crow. How was he going to explain this to River Fox's father Chief Wolf Killer? River Fox, like most of the men in the war party he led, was in his early twenties. His father and many on the council advised against raiding the Crow so late in the season, but the young warrior and many of his friends were filled with pride and arrogance and wanted to prove to their elders that they had strong medicine and wanted to make a name for themselves. They paid the ultimate price for their pride.

Out of the sixty members of the war party, half were killed and only ten of the bodies were retrieved. As the raiding party entered the village, Chief Wolf Killer was already standing outside his lodge. From where he was standing, he could see the raid was a failure. Even worse, his son was not among the war party. Before the bodies of the ten Lakota warriors were even taken off their horses, their mothers and wives were already screaming in agony as they mourned their loved ones. Broken Arrow approached his Chief and dismounted.

"Where is my son?" asked Chief Wolf Killer.

"He was killed in battle," said Broken Arrow as he hung his head in shame. "I saw from a distance."

"Did he die well?"

Broken Arrow slightly raised his head to his Chief. "He fought to the end, until the white man buried his tomahawk into his head."

"A white man?" Broken Arrow nodded.

"There was a white man living among the Crow village we raided," he said. "He was big and tall and had white hair."

Chief Wolf Killer nodded. "How many were killed with him?" he asked.

"About half of those who rode with us," answered Broken Arrow. "But we could only retrieve ten of them."

Chief Wolf Killer nodded and dismissed the youth.

As he went inside to inform his wife of their son's death, a hunting party had returned to the village. The party was led by Chief Wolf Killer's daughter Soaring Eagle Woman. As the hunting party returned with two elk and a deer, they could hear the wailing and mourning throughout their village. Chief Wolf Killer signaled his daughter to him. As she quickly dismounted and approached her father, she sensed he had terrible news to give her.

"Come inside, my daughter," he said. "I have grave news to tell you and your mother."

She looked around the village and stared at the raiding party that her brother led a few days ago. When she saw he was not among them, she knew she would never see him again. However, she remained quiet as she followed her father inside.

3

SOARING EAGLE WOMAN

Upon hearing of the death of her brother in battle against the Crow, Soaring Eagle Woman was not just devastated, but in a rage. The fact that River Fox died at the hands of a white man made it even worse. At least according to her. Soaring Eagle Woman had never trusted the *wasichu* (Lakota for white man). Especially since her village encountered the Corps of Discovery attempting to pass through their lands ten years ago. Deep down she sensed that the *wasichu* was bad medicine, and she wasn't alone in her feelings. Her father and brother shared her mistrust and they definitely didn't like what they didn't trust.

Soaring Eagle Woman was not your typical Lakota woman. She was always different from other women, ever since she was a child. She preferred to play and wrestle with the boys, and as she got older, she preferred to hunt with the men. Her parents did not discourage this; in fact, just the opposite. Five years ago, when she had reached fifteen summers, she went on her first horse stealing raid against the Pawnee, one of the Lakota's most hated enemies. Soaring Eagle Woman saved her older brother's life in that raid and managed to capture over fifty Pawnee horses in the process. Since that day, both her brother and father and all the elders on the council accepted her as a warrior woman. She became one of the best and most feared warriors of her people and this brought both honor and pride to her family. Unlike her older brother, though, she was not impulsive or impetuous. And like most warriors who were more experienced than her and her brother, she thought of the people's needs first, before she thought of herself.

Today was different, though. Soaring Eagle Woman and her brother were close, even though they were different in attitudes and behavior. Her brother was now dead and his young wife, Heals Like A Willow, was now a widow with a three-month old son. Because she lived not as a woman but as a man, according to the customs of her people, she could take her brother's widow as her wife and raise his son. Soaring Eagle Woman would deal with that later. Right now she wanted revenge.

After the funeral for those warriors who were killed was concluded, a council was held. Chief Wolf Killer sat at the head of the council. He personally invited his daughter to join, even though women weren't traditionally allowed to sit on the council. After the peace pipe was smoked and passed, Chief Wolf Killer spoke. "I mourn the loss of my son and all those who died with him," he said. "But now is not the time for vengeance, Winter is coming soon and we must prepare for it, for the good of the people."

Most of the council members agreed. Even the young warriors who went on the ill-fated raid against the Crow did not object.

"Father," said Soaring Eagle Woman. "May I speak?"

"Give us your words, my daughter."

"I agree that the people's needs must come first, but my brother's blood cries out for vengeance. I must find this *wasichu* who lives among our enemies and take his life." A look of concern appeared before her father's face. "However, I will help with the village in preparing for the coming winter," she said. "Come spring, I will travel into Crow country and find this white man who lives among the Crow and took my brother's life."

"You shouldn't go by yourself," said Black Bull. He was the village medicine man and was close to Soaring Eagle Woman's family. He also knew she was the kind of person who preferred to hunt and fight alone.

"I won't be going alone, Uncle. Broken Arrow, you saw my brother fall at the hands of this white dog." That was a statement not a question. Broken Arrow nodded. "Then you know what he looks like?"

"I do," answered Broken Arrow. "He is not an enemy to be underestimated. He is big like the bear on its hind legs, and he has white hair."

"Did you say white hair?" exclaimed Black Bull.

"Yes."

"Does that mean anything to you Black Bull?" asked Chief Wolf Killer.

"It just might," answered Black Bull. "About four summers ago, some Lakota warriors from the village of Long Knife were involved in a battle against some Omaha warriors."

Everyone listened to the holy man intently as he told the story. "My wife's brother was in this battle and he told me that there were two white men fighting alongside the Omaha against them," he said. "Both of these white men had white hair and one of them was as big and tall as the grizzly bear on its hind legs."

This intrigued everyone, including Soaring Eagle Woman. "From what he told me this young, but giant white man, with white hair, fought like the grizzly as well. Many Lakota warriors from Long Knife's village died that day."

"Could this be the same *wasichu*?" asked Soaring Eagle Woman.

"Does it matter?" asked Broken Arrow.

Soaring Eagle Woman gave the warrior a look that made him turn white as snow. "It does to me," she said with venom. "I don't just want to kill any *wasichu*, I want to kill the one who took my brother's life and you're going to help me find him."

Broken Arrow was about to object, but the look on the faces of Soaring Eagle Woman, her father, and the entire council told him that would be unwise.

"You are the only person who knows what he looks like, Broken Arrow," said Chief Wolf Killer. "But it has already been agreed that any vengeance raid against this enemy and his Crow allies will have to wait." Everyone grunted in agreement.

"I will ride to my wife's brother's village tomorrow," said Black Bull. "He can tell us about the two white-haired *wasichus* he fought against that day with the Omaha."

"May I ride with you, Uncle?" asked Soaring Eagle Woman.

"You may. I think it would be a good idea if Broken Arrow comes with us as well, don't you agree, Broken Arrow?"

"I will come," said a reluctant Broken Arrow.

"Take some more men with you," said Chief Wolf Killer. "Safety in numbers."

The same warriors who went on the failed raid against the Crow and survived volunteered to accompany Black Bull and Soaring Eagle Woman to Long Knife's village.

After the council dispersed, Chief Wolf Killer pulled his daughter aside. "I loved your brother just as much as I love you, my daughter," he said. "But he was prideful and thought he had strong medicine."

"I know, father," said Soaring Eagle Woman.

"Don't make the same mistake he made," said her father. "From what Broken Arrow told me, your brother died in battle and with honor. When you go and seek out his killer in the spring, try to capture him alive."

"Alive?"

Chief Wolf Killer nodded. "It is only fair that my son's killer should die in our village at our hands."

"I will find him and bring him back alive," said Soaring Eagle Woman. "If I can."

"I know you will," responded her father. "If anyone gets in your way, do what must be done, no matter what."

"Yes, father. No matter what."

4

THE MISSION

MEANWHILE, back at the village of Chief Medicine Hawk, things returned to normal. The village decided that they were moving to their winter quarters, where the Bridger-Teton National Forest now stands. There would be plenty of game there, so the village would not starve. Lazarus and his family would help the village pack and prepare, but they won't be traveling with them. The winter trapping season was upon them, and the beavers' fur was now already thick for the upcoming winter. Lazarus and his wives and son would stay and trap the Bighorn River, while Plain Feather, Hawk Eyes, and Angus White Cloud would travel with the village and stay with them for the winter. It was agreed that they would meet up back at their home in the Silver Bow Valley near the Clark Fork River.

After saying their goodbyes, the village headed south to the Wind River Mountains, while Lazarus, Dark Wind, Mountain Flower and their infant son Amos Winter Hawk, headed east to the Bighorn River. They would trap up and down the river, bringing in many beaver plews. However, they had to be extremely careful. Grizzly bears were still fattening themselves up for the winter and while most were already heading to the high mountains to begin their hibernation, there were bound to be some that were still feasting on berries and other edibles by the river.

On one early October morning, Lazarus was checking his traps when two grizzly cubs appeared out of a thicket not far from him. Their mother was not far behind and she felt he was too close for comfort, so she charged. Fortunately for Lazarus, there was a nearby tree and he managed to run and climb up it as fast as his legs would carry him. The she-grizzly missed his moccasined feet by an inch as he climbed higher and higher up the tree. There was no time to shoot the momma bear with his rifle, so climbing the tree was his only option.

Now whoever said that adult grizzly bears can't climb trees because they are too heavy was either lying or a fool, because Lazarus Buchanan found out the hard way as his eyes were wide as saucers when he saw the she-grizzly beginning to climb after him. There was nowhere else to run or climb, so he took out one of his pistols and fired at point blank range into the left eye of the bear. Grizzly bears were notoriously hard to kill, and this she-grizzly was no exception. The musket ball didn't kill her but definitely slowed her down. With blood spurting out of her left eye, she quickly climbed back down. Suddenly another gunshot rang out and a musket ball hit her in her side as she was climbing down. This caused her to fall at least ten feet before she hit the ground. Lazarus looked up and saw his wives at a distance. It was Mountain Flower who had fired the shot from her Pennsylvania rifle. The she-grizzly was down, but not out. With only one eye and a bullet wound on her side, she stood on her hind legs and roared.

"Run!" shouted Lazarus. But the women ignored him. Dark Wind fired her Harper's Ferry rifle as Mountain Flower quickly reloaded. Dark Wind's bullet found its mark, hitting the she-grizzly in the neck. The beast was back on all fours and was about to charge at the women. Lazarus took out his other pistol and fired, hitting the beast in the rump. Sensing the threat from behind, the momma grizzly turned back to the tree and tried to climb it again, but she couldn't see out of her left eye and was coughing up blood. With her rifle reloaded, Mountain Flower fired again, this time hitting the bear in the shoulder. The beast went into a hysterical rage, not knowing how to combat the threat that was coming at her from all sides.

Dark Wind had reloaded her rifle and fired at the momma grizzly, this time hitting a lung. The grizzly gave out one last defiant roar, before slowly crawling back to the edge of the river and collapsed. Her two cubs were hiding back in the thicket, while Lazarus climbed down. With his own Harper's Ferry rifle in hand, he slowly approached the dead she grizzly and fired into her side, just to make sure she was dead. Dark Wind and Mountain Flower, with their rifles reloaded, stood next to their husband and fired into the she grizzly. All three were satisfied that she was dead. Little Amos Winter Hawk, who was in his cradleboard on his mother's back, was crying hysterically. His father gently stroked his cheek and sang an old Scottish lullaby to calm him down. It had the intended effect.

"Why didn't you run like I told you to?" he asked.

"We are family," said Dark Wind. "We do not abandon each other."

"But you could have been killed."

"So could you, if we left you to your fate," said Mountain Flower.

"We made a vow, husband," added Dark Wind. "Every danger we face, every enemy we encounter, we will face them together."

Lazarus couldn't argue with that. "That, maybe," he said. "But you two had me scared for a minute. I mean what if that momma grizzly succeeded in coming after you?"

"She didn't, husband," said Mountain Flower. "That is all that matters."

Lazarus just nodded as he and the women reloaded their weapons. Lazarus looked up and saw the grizzly cubs at a distance. "I don't suppose there is anything we could do for them?"

Both women looked at the cubs and just shook their heads. "They are too young to survive without their mother," said Dark Wind. "It is in the Creator's hands."

"It's a shame we had to kill their mother," said Lazarus.

"It was either you or her, husband," responded Mountain Flower. "At least we have some fresh meat and bear grease."

"Aye," said Lazarus. With their mother dead, the cubs ran in the opposite direction. Lazarus hoped that they would survive, but from what he saw, the cubs didn't appear to be even a year old. For them to survive would be a miracle indeed.

Meanwhile in the Black Hills, near where Sundance, Wyoming, now stands, Black Bull, Soaring Eagle Woman, Broken Arrow, and some of the Lakota warriors from their village arrived at the village of Long Knife. They paid their respects to Chief Long Knife, explaining to him that they came to see Spotted Cloud, who was Black Bull's brother-in-law. Spotted Cloud was in his late thirties, just a couple of years younger than Black Bull. He welcomed his sister's husband with open arms, however, he was a little surprised to see him this late in the season.

"You look well, Black Bull," he said.

"As do you," responded Black Bull. "You know Soaring Eagle Woman, daughter of Chief Wolf Killer?"

"Of course," smiled the warrior. "Words of your strong medicine and your battles against our enemies are spoken highly around our campfires."

"I thank you for the kind words, Uncle," said Soaring Eagle Woman. "But I come bearing bad news and we need your help."

"I will try to help you as much as I can," said Spotted Cloud. "Give me your words."

"My brother River Fox was killed on a raid against the Crow over twelve sleeps ago," said Soaring Eagle Woman. "But he was not killed by a Crow, but by a *wasichu*."

"A *wasichu* you say?"

Soaring Eagle Woman nodded. "Broken Arrow was on this raid and witnessed my brother's death at the hands of this white dog."

"He was big like the grizzly bear on its hind legs," said Broken Arrow. "And his hair was white, like the snow."

Spotted Cloud's eyes were wide as his interests piqued.

"We are told that you and some of your warriors encountered

such a man when you fought against the Omaha four summers ago," said Black Bull.

Spotted Cloud nodded. "This *wasichu* with the hair white as snow," he said. "Did he appear young?"

"Yes," answered Broken Arrow. "He didn't appear to be that much older than me or River Fox."

"Was there an older *wasichu* with him?" asked Spotted Cloud. "Whose hair was also white as snow, but not as tall?"

"No," answered Broken Arrow.

Spotted Cloud was in deep thought for a moment. "I remember as if it was yesterday," he said. "We had stumbled upon a hunting party of Omaha and we thought it would be easy for us to kill them all and take their horses since we outnumbered them."

"What happened?" asked Soaring Eagle Woman.

"We didn't know that there was an Omaha village nearby," answered Spotted Cloud. "Also, we didn't count on these two white-haired *wasichus* coming in against us, either." Spotted Cloud was quiet again, before he continued on. "The battle was fierce, but I remember the younger *wasichu*. He came to the aid of an Omaha warrior by running down three of my best warriors. I have never seen anything like it before or since, and from one man."

"Sounds like the one we encountered among the Crow," said Broken Arrow.

"The Omaha were reinforced and we had no choice but to retreat," said Spotted Cloud. "But before we retreated, I saw my best friend Crazy Hawk struck down by this young *wasichu*."

"Could it be the same person?" asked Soaring Eagle Woman.

"There are not a lot of *wasichus* out here, but that could change and that is what worries me," said Spotted Cloud. "It probably is him."

"How can you be so sure?" asked Black Bull.

"I have heard stories around the campfires," answered Spotted Cloud. "About a white-haired *wasichu* who is friends with the Omaha, but lives among the Crow, Flathead, and Nez Perce."

"All are our enemies," said Soaring Eagle Woman.

"This is true," responded Spotted Cloud. "But this man has strong medicine. Even the Blackfeet have some respect for him."

"Since when do the Blackfeet respect any *wasichu*?" scoffed Broken Arrow.

"Since three of their most feared warriors were killed by this man in hand-to-hand combat," answered Spotted Cloud. "One of them was Black Thunder and his son Lightning Strikes." Everyone's faces lit up in surprise.

"This man killed Black Thunder and Lightning Strikes?" exclaimed Soaring Eagle Woman.

"So I have heard," said Spotted Cloud.

"Apparently this *wasichu* has strong medicine and must not be underestimated," said Black Bull.

"I agree, Uncle," responded Soaring Eagle Woman. "But it doesn't change the fact that he killed my brother and I will search the ends of the earth to have his scalp!"

"You must be smart, Soaring Eagle Woman," said Spotted Cloud. "This enemy has friends, even among the Flathead, since he helped push the Hudson's Bay Company out of their country last spring."

"He is an enemy of the Hudson's Bay Company?" asked Black Bull. "This could be useful."

"I don't trust any *wasichu*," said Soaring Eagle Woman. "Whether they are from the north or the east, I don't trust them and I don't like what I don't trust."

Both Black Bull and Spotted Cloud laughed. "Just like your father," said Black Bull.

"What will you do?" asked Spotted Cloud.

"We will help our village get ready for the upcoming winter," said Soaring Eagle Woman. "I promised my father that I would."

"Good," said Spotted Cloud. "Then after?" "In the spring, I will travel into Crow country and find this *wasichu* and bring him back to my village to face justice."

"If it pleases you, Soaring Eagle Woman," said Spotted Cloud. "I would like to accompany you and help you on this endeavor."

"You would be welcomed, Uncle."

"One more thing," said Spotted Cloud. "The *wasichu* that we seek, I am told the Omaha have given him a name and he is known by that name."

"Oh?" said Black Bull. "That name is?"

"He is called White Bear.

5

VISIONS

Lazarus and his family continued to trap the upper Bighorn River until the beginning of November. They brought in over 500 beaver plews, which wasn't a bad haul. Sensing winter coming around the corner, they packed up and traveled west to their home in the Silver Bow Valley. There they would cache their plews and winter until the spring. The meat and grease from the she-grizzly was a welcomed commodity, for the women would grind some of the meat into jerky, while the grease would be used for cooking.

Jerky, whether it was from buffalo, deer, elk, moose, or bear, was highly useful among both Indians and trappers alike. Originally called pemmican, it was a mixture of dried meat, tallow, and some-times dried berries. A calorie rich food, it could either be used in prepared meals or eaten raw. This high calorie food offered great energy for both trappers and Indians during travel and hunting, when food might be scarce.

When they weren't traveling, Lazarus and his family would tan the bear hide and make pemmican from some of the meat. They continued to travel west until a snowstorm stopped them at the Yellowstone's Clarks Fork River, near the Beartooth Mountains. They hunkered down and took shelter before the storm got worse. Lazarus hobbled the horses and pack animals, being sure to clear some of the snow away for the animals to be able to eat the grass. When everyone was settled, Dark Wind breastfed Little Amos, while Mountain Flower managed to get the coffee started.

Lazarus brought in the firewood so their tipi would be warm that night. While they still had plenty of bear meat and pemmican, Lazarus felt the need to go hunting.

"Once the storm clears, I'm going to see if I can get some game," he said.

"There is no need," said Dark Wind. "We should have enough food to last us until we reach home."

"I agree," said Mountain Flower. "You should hunt only when necessary."

"And you ladies think it is not necessary now?"

Both women nodded.

"When we reach the Silver Bow Valley," said Dark Wind. "There'll be plenty of game to hunt and last us for the rest of the winter."

"If you think that's best," said Lazarus.

Dark Wind finished feeding Amos and passed him to his father. "Now is the time for you to be a father to your son."

Lazarus smiled and took his son from his mother. As he gently put him on his chest and patted his back to burp him, Lazarus saw some sadness in Mountain Flower's eyes. He knew what it was and so did Dark Wind. Mountain Flower had been living with them for over two years now and she still couldn't understand why she had not gotten pregnant. She wanted to have Lazarus' baby and give Amos a sibling. Both Dark Wind and Lazarus tried to comfort her.

"Be patient, my sister," said Dark Wind. "In due time, you will have White Bear's baby."

"I wish I had your confidence," said Mountain Flower.

"Don't lose hope," said Lazarus. "You can't, not after everything we have been through."

For the first time Mountain Flower smiled. "Since when did you become so wise husband?"

Lazarus just shrugged. "You can learn a thing or two from Aunt Plain Feather and her parents," he said. "Dark Wind's parents, too."

With that, the women giggled as Mountain Flower poured some coffee for Dark Wind and Lazarus before pouring some for herself.

After midnight, as the snowstorm managed to calm down, Lazarus slept comfortably under his buffalo robe between his two naked wives. Amos Winter Hawk slept soundly and warmly in his rabbit fur cradleboard, waking up only once because he'd soiled himself and needed to be changed. After that it was an uneventful night as the family slept soundly.

Suddenly, something had awakened Lazarus. He opened his eyes and listened. The storm had quieted down and nothing had spooked the horses, but something was bugging the trapper. He lifted his head slightly and was shocked to see a man sitting on the other side of the fire, which had died down a bit. Lazarus tried to wake his wives and almost went for his pistol, when he realized that they were no longer there.

"What the Hell?"

"Relax, lad," said the stranger. Lazarus suddenly recognized the voice of his late uncle, Amos MacKinnon.

"I know I'm dreaming," he said.

"Aye," said Uncle Amos. "I have just come to remind you to beware of the warrior woman."

"What warrior woman?" asked Lazarus.

"Beware!"

Suddenly, Lazarus awoke in a sweat, waking both his wives.

"Lazarus," said Dark Wind. "Are you well?"

"A dream," he answered. "It was a dream."

"What kind of dream?" asked Mountain Flower.

"I saw my Uncle Amos," he said.

Both women's interest piqued. "Is it the same vision?" asked Dark Wind.

Lazarus nodded. "He keeps telling me, beware of the warrior woman."

"We have a new enemy," said Mountain Flower. Both Dark Wind and Lazarus knew that was a statement not a question.

"But who?" asked Lazarus. "Who is this warrior woman and why is she our enemy?"

"When we reach my people we should discuss this with Two Bears," said Dark Wind.

Two Bears was the Medicine Man or Holy Man of Dark Wind's village and a close friend of her family. Lazarus remembered the man and thought very highly of him since he'd tried to save his Uncle Amos from death.

"When we reach our cabins, we will cache our plews and then seek out your village," said Lazarus. "I will consult with Two Bears."

Both Dark Wind and Mountain Flower kissed their husband on each side of his face as he held them both close to him and all three laid back down.

"God, please help me protect my family," he quietly said to himself.

Meanwhile, back at Bear Mountain, Soaring Eagle Woman also had a vision of her own. She had just awakened in a cold sweat. Her father, Chief Wolf Killer, was already awake.

"What troubles you, my daughter?" he asked.

"I had a vision, father," she said. "I saw him."

"Who?"

"White Bear. I had him in my clutches."

"He escaped?" asked her father.

"No. Two women appeared."

"What did they look like?"

"One was Flathead and the other was Nez Perce. They were armed with the *wasichu*'s *mazawakan* (Lakota for rifle)."

"What did these women do?" asked her father.

"I don't know. I woke up and the vision was gone." She was quiet for a moment. "Father, I saw the fire in their eyes, though," she finally said. "I think these women are his wives."

"You should consult with Black Bull about this. This changes everything."

"It changes nothing," she said quietly but with some venom. "I will hunt him in the spring and bring him back to face justice as promised, and I will not let anything or anyone stand in my way."

"You are a warrior, my daughter," said Chief Wolf Killer. "Since when do warriors make war on women?"

She was about to answer, but then stopped herself. What her father said was true, but she wanted revenge on the white man who killed her brother. If he did have two wives, who obviously would fight to protect him, then what could she do?

"I will consult with Black Bull," she finally said.

6

TROUBLE AT HOME

THE SNOW STORM lasted only a day. The next day, Lazarus and his family packed up and continued their journey west to Silver Bow Valley. It would take another couple of days to get there, depending on the weather and barring any delays. As they were traveling, both Lazarus and his wives sensed that they were being watched and followed. They continued to travel from the Yellowstone region, but went south to avoid Three Forks, which was in Blackfoot country. They traveled through what is now Yellowstone National Park in northwestern Wyoming, before finding their way back north into Flathead country. By the second week of November, they'd made it home to Silver Bow Creek.

While winter came early in the mountains, the weather was mild by the time Lazarus and his family arrived at their cabins. Heavily armed, they checked inside to make sure they didn't have any unwanted visitors of both the four-legged and two-legged variety. When all was deemed clear, the women started sweeping and cleaning inside their home. Left to sit for long periods, the cabin accumulated dust on just about every surface.

Lazarus went to check the smokehouse and was relieved that there were no rodents, snakes, or other critters trying to find a warm place to sleep for the winter. There was still some bear meat left, but not enough to see them through the winter. After Lazarus hung the rest of the meat in the smokehouse, he planned on going hunting in the morning. Suddenly he stopped as his sixth sense came into play. Lazarus dove to the ground, avoiding a Blackfoot arrow as it harmlessly *thunked* into the door of the smokehouse.

Lazarus managed to get up in time to see three Blackfoot warriors, all painted for war, coming straight towards him. He immediately pulled his pistols, cocked them, quickly aimed, and fired, taking down two of the warriors. The Blackfoot warrior that fired the arrow and missed managed to halt and nock another arrow, but before he could fire, a gunshot rang out from behind him and he found a new hole in his chest before he fell to the earth, never to rise again.

Dark Wind was holding her Kentucky rifle, which was smoking. Lazarus nodded his thanks to his wife, before quickly reloading his pistols and going to check on the two Blackfoot warriors he'd gunned down. Only one was still alive, but not for long. He was gut shot and knew his time was near. Lazarus turned him over and pointed one of his pistols at him. He was joined by both his wives, with their reloaded rifles aimed at the dying warrior.

"Cover me," he said. Both women nodded. Lazarus put his pistols away in his belt and used sign language. "Why did you attack us?"

The Blackfoot warrior, hatred gleaming in eyes, just spat before answering in sign, "You are White Bear. We wanted your scalp."

"You would attack a lone man and his family?" asked Lazarus in disgust. "For what, honor? Glory?"

The dying Blackfoot just chuckled as he began to get weak. "I will be dead soon," he said. "And you and your women will not be long following me."

"How many warriors came with you?" asked Lazarus in sign. The warrior remained silent. Lazarus decided to improvise. He stuck two of his fingers into the dying warrior's wounded abdomen and proceeded to pull out his guts. The warrior tried to fight, but both Dark Wind and Mountain Flower were standing on his arms and chest to keep him from resisting as their husband tortured him for answers. The warrior was coughing up blood and screaming in agonizing pain at the same time.

When Lazarus stopped for a minute, he signed to the dying man. "Tell me what I want to know and I will end your pain." Lazarus nodded to his wives to take their feet off the man.

"There were two others. They rode to get more warriors when we saw you and followed you here."

Lazarus and his wives' eyes were wide as saucers. This told them that Blackfeet were in the area and searching for them. Without hesitation, Lazarus took out his Arkansas toothpick and slit the man's throat.

"This is not good," he said. "Take our son and find Chief Snake Killer's village and tell him we need help."

"What will you do?" asked Dark Wind.

"I'm going to take these three bodies to their friends as a warning," answered Lazarus.

"Not by yourself you're not," said Mountain Flower.

"Now is not the time to argue," said Lazarus. "A Blackfoot war party is in the area, which means we are in danger. By the time I find them, you should be able to find Chief Snake Killer's warriors and have them follow me."

The women knew that they were fighting a losing argument. When Lazarus puts his mind to something, especially in defense of his family, his mind was set.

"We will do as you say, husband," said Dark Wind. "But don't be reckless. If you find the Blackfoot war party, wait for my people."

Lazarus smiled at both of his brides. "Don't you worry," he said. "I'm not about to turn you into widows, not if I can help it."

"Be serious, Lazarus," said Mountain Flower.

"I am serious. Now, hurry and go. I will take care of these bodies."

Both Dark Wind and Mountain Flower quickly took little Amos, mounted up, and rode out to find the Flathead village of Chief Snake Killer. As they left, Lazarus gathered the three Blackfoot bodies and tied each of them to a horse. He had a plan and he prayed to God that it would work. But, he would need help from his in-laws and friends from Snake Killer's village. While he didn't like killing, if the rest of the Blackfoot war party found where he and his family lived, then he would have no choice but to wipe them all out. He prayed it would not come to that, but he was also a realist and knew it probably would. Either way, his family's safety was all that mattered to him. Nothing more, nothing less.

7

REINFORCEMENTS AND A WARNING

As HIS FAMILY rode north by northwest to find the Flatheads, Lazarus tied the Blackfoot bodies to each of his pack horses. Heavily armed, he rode east towards the Missouri River. South of that was Three Forks, which was in Blackfoot country. But Lazarus was not planning to ride that far. He knew that the Blackfoot war party was close. Too close to his home, which was too close for comfort. It began to snow a little bit before he found horse tracks. Lazarus dismounted to examine them. They led away from his home, so he followed them.

He didn't have far to go, when he spotted the war party and their camp. The warriors were getting themselves ready, painting their faces and their horses. Lazarus just shook his head as he watched from his hiding place. "All this to kill one man and his family," he said to himself. He slowly backed away into the forest and found a small clearing. This is where he put his plan into motion. He took the three Blackfoot bodies and hung them on a tree, but not before carving the shape of a bear claw into each of their chests as a warning.

With his work done, he quickly, but quietly rode out of the area. Heading back home with the Blackfoot war party still in the area was not an option. He rode about a mile away from their camp, to a small clearing. He was halfway in distance between the Clark Fork River and the Missouri River. He hobbled his horses and waited behind a downed tree. He had three of his rifles ready and loaded as he waited.

The Blackfoot war party mounted up and rode west, but not far from where they camped they ran smack dab into where Lazarus had hung the bodies of their three comrades. Stone Bear, the leader of the war party, rode up to the bodies and examined them. He was followed by the two warriors that returned to the camp to tell them about where they found White Bear and his family. Once they saw the bear claw shape carved into the flesh of their friends, they knew who was responsible.

"This is White Bear's doing," said Prairie Fire. He was one of the two warriors that returned to tell Stone Bear about the whereabouts of the home of their enemy. Stone Bear nodded. He noticed that none of his friends were scalped or mutilated in any way.

"He knows we are here," he said. "He did this as a warning."

"A warning?" said a confused Prairie Fire.

"A warning for us," responded Stone Bear. "To stay away."

"He is just one man," said another warrior. "A white man no less."

Stone Bear turned around on his horse and looked at his warriors. "Do not underestimate this one white man," he said. "If what all of us have heard about him is true, he is no fool." He turned back to the bodies once again, before he spoke again. "Prairie Fire," he said. "Take two volunteers and take our three friends home for burial."

"What about White Bear?" asked Prairie Fire.

"Leave him to us," said Stone Bear.

The young warrior did what he was told and got two volunteers to help him take the bodies back to their people.

Stone Bear addressed the rest of the war party. "We must tread carefully," he said. "White Bear is obviously a cunning enemy and knows that we are hunting him." His warriors whooped and cheered in agreement. As they continued east, Stone Bear had Red Beak in the lead. Red Beak was the best tracker in the group and saw Lazarus' horse tracks. The war party followed the tracks of their quarry to a small clearing. At that moment a gunshot rang out, but the bullet harmless hit the ground, kicking up dust in the horse's face, frightening them for the moment.

As soon as they got their horses under control, the war party saw who they were after. Stone Bear was correct. Lazarus was waiting for them. He ordered his men to halt, for their enemy had the high ground.

"Wait here," he said. "Anyone who fires or charges will answer to me." Stone Bear slowly rode up and held up his hand, giving the sign of peace. Lazarus could see that the Blackfoot leader wanted to parley, so he signaled him over. He stood and stepped over the log he was hiding behind. He was still armed with a rifle in a ready to shoot position, but he let Stone Bear know he was willing to talk.

Stone Bear rode his horse until he stopped ten feet from Lazarus. He looked the young white trapper up and down and was impressed. "Are you the one called White Bear?" he asked in sign.

"I am."

"I am Stone Bear."

"Why do you seek me out?" asked Lazarus.

"You are the enemy of my people. You have killed many of my warriors."

"This is true. But they tried to kill me and many of my friends."

Stone Bear nodded his understanding.

"I have no quarrel with your people," said Lazarus. "I do not tread into your lands to trap the flat tail, out of respect to your medicine. All I want is for me and my family to be left alone."

The Blackfoot warrior gave a smirk. "You are truly an honorable enemy," he said. "Which is why I have to speak to you."

"My ears are open."

"Surrender yourself to me and my warriors and you will be given a quick death."

Lazarus would have laughed if he thought the Blackfoot leader was joking. "You said I was an honorable enemy."

"You are still an enemy. I give you my word that no harm will come to your family."

"I will not turn my wives into widows voluntarily. If you and your warriors leave here now and do not return, there will be no bloodshed."

"If blood will be shed today, it will be yours."

"I will take you and some of your warriors with me," responded Lazarus.

"You may have the high ground, but you are still one man."

"I won't be for long."

Stone Bear knew what the trapper meant by that, but thought he was bluffing. However, he was no fool. Lazarus did have the high ground and a lot of warriors would die trying to take his scalp before they overtook him.

"I like you, White Bear. If only you had been born a Blackfoot, you would be a great warrior of my people."

Lazarus nodded his thanks. Both men knew the parley was done and that a fight was coming. Lazarus allowed the warrior to leave and return to his men, while he returned to his defensive position.

When Stone Bear returned to his warriors, he instructed them to scatter and outflank Lazarus Buchanan.

"Why don't we just go in and charge?" asked one of his warriors. "He is only one white man."

"Because that is what he expects us to do. He has the high ground and can take us out one by one."

"Are there others?" asked another warrior.

"He told me that he is expecting others. We are in Flathead country. While we outnumber him now, he may have friends that are coming, which is why we must capture him quickly, take him back to our village, and kill him slowly."

The rest of the war party thought their leader's plan was sound and made sense. They followed his orders and scattered, attempting to outflank Lazarus' position.

Using his spyglass, Lazarus could see the war party and what they were trying to do. While he did have the high ground, he couldn't be in more than one place. He prayed his wives had found Chief Snake Killer's village and were on their way back with reinforcements.

The war party numbered at least fifty warriors. Ten warriors volunteered to charge straight ahead to attack, distracting Lazarus in order to give the other warriors a chance to maneuver and flank him. Their plan worked. As the ten warriors charged, Lazarus let them get close enough in firing range before he fired the first shot. One warrior went down before Lazarus took his second rifle and fired the second shot. When the second warrior went down, the remaining eight scattered. While Lazarus quickly reloaded his first two rifles, he heard war whoops from behind him.

"Those bastards couldn't have gotten to me already," he said to himself. But suddenly he looked up from his position and what was coming before him brought a smile to his face. There were over a hundred Flathead warriors emerging from around the bend. Led by Lazarus' father-in-law Plenty Hawk, they charged right at their long-time hated enemies, the Blackfeet.

Seeing that the tables had turned, and that he and his warriors were outnumbered, Stone Bear immediately called a retreat. Some of the Blackfoot warriors that had scattered to outflank Lazarus were overtaken and cut down by the Flathead. Lazarus immediately went to his horses and mounted his black stallion to quickly join his Flathead brothers. As he was leaving his position, he was pleased to find Dark Wind and her brother Lone Falcon riding next to him to chase their enemy back to their own country.

Once Stone Bear and his warriors left the area, the Flathead gave up the chase and returned to the scene of the battlefield. Out of the fifty Blackfoot warriors, only six were killed and two were captured. Lazarus convinced his father-in-law and brother-in-law to let the two prisoners go, but with a warning. No one argued, even when Lazarus asked the rescue party not to scalp or mutilate the six Blackfoot warriors who were killed.

Lazarus approached the two prisoners. "Tell Stone Bear and the rest of your people," he signed, "that any enemy who treads into the lands of the Flathead and the home of White Bear, will not be seen or heard from again."

The two prisoners looked at each other and then at Lazarus and the Flathead warriors. They were allowed to leave and give their leader the message.

"We will gather the bodies of your friends," signed Lazarus. "Tell Stone Bear that he and his warriors can come and retrieve them, but once they have done that, they must return to their home country or they will suffer the same fate." Both warriors nodded their understanding and left.

After the prisoners left, Dark Wind ran to her husband and hugged her. "For a minute there I was afraid that you would be a widow," said Lazarus.

"I thank the Creator that I am not," responded Dark Wind.

"Mountain Flower and Amos?"

"They are safe in the village."

Lazarus gave his wife a passionate kiss before greeting his father-in-law and brother-in-law.

"Had you not come when you did..." he said. But he didn't finish the sentence.

"You are still here, my son," said Plenty Hawk. "That is all that matters." Lazarus clasped arms with his father-in-law and did the same with Lone Falcon. A change in the weather was coming and it started to snow.

"We best get home," said Lazarus. No one disagreed.

8

THE LONG WINTER

As FALL soon turned into winter, Lazarus and his family had quickly settled in after the battle with the Blackfeet. Their cabins were not far from the Flathead village of Chief Snake Killer, so many a morning some of the warriors, led by Lone Falcon, would often come and visit to invite Lazarus to hunt. The trapper was always overjoyed to hunt with his brother-in-law and friends, especially when the weather permitted. Despite the harsh winters that came to the Silver Bow Valley, there was still plenty of game to hunt around the Clark Fork and Bitterroot Rivers.

Lazarus, Lone Falcon, and the Flathead hunting party traveled west to the Bitterroot River and spent the next couple of days hunting up and down it and its surrounding areas. They managed to bring back two mule deer, a full-grown bull moose, and a yearling elk by the end of the week. This was more than enough meat to feed the entire village and Lazarus' family for at least a month. Lazarus stored some of the meat in his smokehouse so it wouldn't spoil. Despite the success of the hunt, everyone knew there would have to be more hunts, because the winters in the mountains were long and fierce, and starvation was a real threat.

While he would hunt, Lazarus would also trap the Bitterroot River and its tributaries for beaver. The river itself was eighty-four miles long, flowing northward through the Bitterroot Valley and eastward to the confluence of the Clark Fork and Blackfoot Rivers. It was still the middle of November, but despite winter coming early in the mountains, that didn't stop Lazarus and his family from trapping when the weather permitted. He would bring in almost 100 plews to add to his 500 before the weather turned for the worst.

By the time December hit, the winter trapping season was over. Lazarus cached his winter beaver plews and would go hunting for game. While his family still had enough meat in the smokehouse, a man never knew when he or his family would need extra meat. So every couple of days, when the weather permitted, Lazarus and his family would travel and hunt the surrounding areas in their valley. They managed to kill a mountain buffalo cow and a few days later a full-grown bull elk. Enough meat to last the entire winter of 1814, until possibly the end of January 1815. The family also had plenty of vegetables that they grew in their garden around the cabins from seeds they bought from their last trip to St. Louis.

Every now and then, Lazarus would go fishing in the snow and catch cutthroat trout to help supplement the meat from buffalo, elk, deer, and bear. When he was hunting, Lazarus would spend time repairing his beaver traps, fixing and cleaning his guns and his wives' guns, and sharpening their knives and tomahawks. The frontier was not a place where people who were complacent survived long. Lazarus remembered the lessons his late uncle taught him and he learned them well.

However, he was still bothered by the warning his uncle gave him in his visions. "Beware of the warrior woman." This really started to concern Lazarus and the first chance he got, he was going to ride to the village and consult with Two Bears. Lazarus hoped that these dreams were exactly that, dreams, but Indians took great stock in them as a message from the Creator.

Come to think of it, so do we white people, Lazarus thought to himself. He remembered from his family's Holy Bible examples of how God spoke to individuals through dreams. Lazarus's favorite tale from the Bible was the story of Joseph, the son of Jacob. Lazarus remembered how God gave Joseph a message through his dreams and the gift to interpret dreams, which Joseph used to not only save his family, but an entire nation from complete starvation.

Lazarus never forgot about his Presbyterian Christian upbringing. While he never considered himself religious by any means, he still believed in God and the Holy Bible. While he never took one with him, when he'd left home four years ago, he'd hoped to buy or trade for one the next time he and his family traveled to St. Louis. Both Dark Wind and Mountain Flower were curious about their husband's Christian faith. He often shared it with them, when they asked about it, but he never forced it on them or behaved in a way that his faith was superior to theirs. In fact, Lazarus believed that who he called Jesus Christ and who most of the tribes call the Creator or the Great Mystery, were one in the same. Most white Christians and some Indians would denounce this, however, from Lazarus' memory of his reading of the Bible, he found that Christianity and the religious beliefs of most of the tribes he had encountered were not that different. In fact, he felt that if most whites, especially those claiming to be Christians, would let go of their racist and narrow-minded view of the world, they might realize how much they had in common with both Indians and Black people, who both had been treated terribly by Lazarus' kind.

This is what hurt Lazarus, feeling and knowing how his blood relatives back in Delaware would treat his wives, son, his Uncle's widow and his little cousin. While he had enemies among the Blackfeet and Lakota, most of the tribes, such as the Crow, Omaha, Flathead, and Nez Perce, had not only treated him with kindness, but they had adopted him as one of their own. It amazed Lazarus, as he was bouncing his son on his knee one evening, that despite his wives and his aunt knowing what his people were like, they still hoped to one day meet his family from the east. This was running through

Lazarus' mind, as was the thought of who this warrior woman was, if she truly existed and was a threat to his family.

"Something on your mind, husband?" asked Mountain Flower. She was setting the table as Dark Wind was almost done cooking dinner.

"A lot is on my mind. My dreams are one of the things."

"Are you still having them?" asked Dark Wind.

"Not since we left the Bighorn River a few moons ago. First chance I get, when the weather permits, we will go see your people and I will consult with Two Bears."

"They are your people, too, husband."

Lazarus smiled. "I keep forgetting," he said. "But this warrior woman, if she is real and is a threat, then I need to face her, but hopefully I won't have to."

"What do you mean you hope you won't have to?" asked Mountain Flower.

Lazarus was quiet for a moment as he laid Little Amos on his shoulder and patted his back a little. "In all the years that you have known me," he said, "when have you known me to hit a woman, let alone kill one?"

Both women were silent for a minute, then they realized their husband had never done such a thing.

"We have never even heard of you committing such an act," said Mountain Flower.

"It's not who you are," added Dark Wind.

"Exactly!" said Lazarus. "Now we might have a new enemy who is a woman and possibly wants to kill me."

Mountain Flower approached Lazarus and sat next to him, gently placing her hand on his leg. "Whoever she is, husband, you will not face her alone."

"You won't even have to kill her in defending us," added Dark Wind.

"I won't?" asked Lazarus.

"No, because we will kill her defending you."

Lazarus looked at both of his wives and knew they weren't joking.

"I will not allow you ladies to put yourselves in danger like that. Not even for me."

"We can and we will," said Mountain Flower defiantly.

"We are a family," added Dark Wind. "We will face this new enemy together and not apart."

Lazarus knew better than to argue with his wives. He knew they had his best interests at heart and they knew he had their best interest at heart. "Maybe you're right," he said. "I just want you and our son to be safe, that's all that matters to me."

"We want the same for you," said Dark Wind. "The only way for that to happen is if we face everything together as a family."

Lazarus looked back and forth between his wives and smiled. "How did I get so lucky?"

"When the Creator puts good people in your life who love you, it isn't luck, my husband," said Dark Wind. "It is a blessing."

Meanwhile, in the winter camp of Chief Wolf Killer, near the Badlands and the Cheyenne River, Soaring Eagle Woman had just returned from a successful hunt. She and some warriors found a herd of buffalo and the village managed to take down enough animals to last the rest of the winter, despite the weather. The Great Mystery has smiled on the people, but Soaring Eagle Woman was troubled. As she sat in her lodge, she thought of the vision she'd had a couple of moons ago. The vision of the white man she sought out. In it, he was somehow protected by two women, a Flathead and a Nez Perce. Who were they and what was he to them? Were they his wives? If so, did they care enough about him that they would fight to protect him? All this was running through her mind during the entire winter.

While she was deep in thought, there was a scratch on her door flap. "Come in," she said. The flap was lifted and Spotted Cloud and Black Bull entered. Soaring Eagle Woman had told the medicine man about her vision and her thoughts. His advice was that she continue to tread cautiously and he was planning to tell her again now.

"How are you feeling, Soaring Eagle Woman?" asked Black Bull.

"I'm fine, Uncle. The winter has been long."

"And it is not over yet," said Black Bull. "But Wakan Tanka smiles on us with another successful hunt and enough food for the rest of the winter."

"This is true, and for that I am grateful."

"As we were talking on the way over here," said Spotted Cloud, "Black Bull and I agreed that we see no reason why we can't go and find your brother's killer now."

"It is the middle of winter," said Soaring Eagle Woman.

"This is true," responded Spotted Cloud. "But we can use that to our advantage."

"Spotted Cloud is right," said Black Bull. "This White Bear is probably wintering with the Crow, or the Flathead and Nez Perce, maybe. Either way, he probably believes he is safe until the spring."

"He will never expect an enemy to come searching for him in the middle of winter," added Spotted Cloud.

Soaring Eagle Woman was in thought for a moment. She thought that advice was sound, and strategically it would be an excellent plan. The people had already been taken care of and there was enough meat for the rest of the winter. Going to find and hunt White Bear now was sound and made sense.

"You are right, my Uncles. I will inform my father and I will leave in a few days."

"You mean *we* will leave in a few days," said Spotted Cloud. "Remember, you should not hunt this *wasichu* by yourself and Broken Arrow is the only one who knows what he looks like."

"You're right, Uncle," said Soaring Eagle Woman. "I am sorry."

"No apologies are necessary," said Spotted Cloud. "You will have justice for your brother, but you must be patient."

"And smart," added Black Bull. "Remember, this *wasichu* has strong medicine. He must not be underestimated."

"I will remember that, Uncle."

"Now come, my child," said Black Bull. "The food is ready and waiting to be devoured, for a great warrior must never go through the day with an empty stomach."

For the first time, Soaring Eagle Woman smiled while Spotted

Cloud chuckled. Deep down she was excited. She would be leaving soon to hunt down the white man called White Bear.

"Enjoy your comfort now, White Bear, wherever you are," she said to herself. "For I am coming for you and there will be no place for you to hide from me!"

9

THE HUNT BEGINS

A COUPLE OF DAYS LATER, Soaring Eagle Woman, Spotted Cloud, Broken Arrow, and a few warriors left their village and headed west into Crow country. They followed the Cheyenne River into the Belle Fourche River, before heading north into the Powder River region. They came across a Cheyenne hunting party and parleyed with them, since the two tribes were allies. The Cheyenne hunting party had heard of the white man known as White Bear and based on the information they'd heard, he was an adopted Crow, Flathead, and Nez Perce. The Crow village he was part of was the village of Medicine Hawk.

"Your best chance of finding this white-haired man is Medicine Hawk's winter camp near the Bighorn Mountains," said the Cheyenne leader in sign.

"We thank you," responded Soaring Eagle Woman. She gave the leader some tobacco as a sign of gratitude before she and the Lakota warriors went on their way. As they were riding, Spotted Cloud rode next to her, to have a chat.

"The Bighorn mountains are a vast area," he said.

"This is true," she responded. "But I have a plan."

"Oh? Would you care to share it?"

Soaring Eagle Woman smiled. "The Crow know where White Bear lives, so once we find the village of Medicine Hawk, we capture a Crow from that village and make him or her tell us."

"Smart plan," said Spotted Cloud.

"Devious, lacking honor, but smart."

"I didn't say that we would kill the Crow," chuckled Soaring Eagle Woman. "Or we could hold the Crow warrior for ransom and let White Bear come to us."

"I like the second plan better," responded Spotted Cloud. "You think he will submit?"

"If he has any sense of honor and cares about the Crow as much as they care about him, he will," answered Soaring Eagle Woman. "But that is the least of my concerns."

"Oh," said Spotted Cloud. "What concerns you more?"

"I don't know if I or Black Bull told you, but I had a vision of White Bear. He was in my clutches, but then two women appeared, one Flathead and the other a Nez Perce."

"What happened next?"

"Nothing. I woke up, but I remember the dream or vision that I had and the fire in these women's eyes was real."

"Well, from what we have been told," said Spotted Cloud, "White Bear lives among the Flathead and Nez Perce, so it is possible these two women are his wives."

"That is the conclusion I came to, which is why I prefer we capture a close ally of White Bear, meaning a Crow."

Spotted Cloud looked at Soaring Eagle Woman. "I have never known you to be afraid of an enemy," he said. "Especially a woman. Never underestimate an enemy?" Spotted Cloud chuckled. "If you were my daughter, Soaring Eagle Woman, I would be the proudest father on earth."

"You honor me, but it is not honor I am after."

"I know," said Spotted Cloud. "You seek vengeance for your brother."

"And I *will* have it. One way or another."

Meanwhile at the village of Chief Snake Killer, Lazarus

Buchanan was consulting with his father-in-law Plenty Hawk, Two Bears, the village Medicine Man, his brother-in-law Lone Falcon, and even his mother-in-law Fighting Bear Woman, about his troubled dreams.

"A warrior woman?" said Two Bears. "Interesting."

"And in your vision, your uncle warned about this warrior woman?" asked Plenty Hawk.

"Yes, Father," answered Lazarus. "Thing is, I don't know what tribe she is from or if she even exists at all."

"If the Creator sent you a warning such as this, White Bear," said Two Bears, "then she exists."

"What am I to do?" asked Lazarus. "My wives don't wish me to face this enemy alone, and I appreciate that, but I don't want them to put themselves in danger, not even for my sake."

"My daughter and Mountain Flower are a lot stronger than you know, White Bear," said Plenty Hawk. "In fact, most women are."

"I take it that is experience talking, Father," said Lazarus. Plenty Hawk smiled and nodded before giving a wink at his wife, Fighting Bear Woman. "In speaking of women," said Lazarus. "That is another problem that bothers me about who this person is."

"Oh?" said Two Bears.

"If this new enemy was a man, I would have no problem hunting him down and removing him as a threat to me and my family. The fact that it is possibly a woman changes everything."

"Why?" asked Lone Falcon.

"Because White Bear doesn't believe in making war on women," said Dark Wind.

"This true?" asked Plenty Hawk.

"My wife speaks with a straight tongue," answered Lazarus. "The way I was raised, you don't hit or harm a woman, for any reason."

"Interesting," said Two Bears. "Are all white men raised like that, or just you?"

"Far as I know, just me. My father and my mother's father always told me that a man who strikes a woman is nothing more than a coward."

"Even if that woman is trying to take your scalp?" asked a surprised Lone Falcon.

Lazarus just shrugged. "I have never been in a position where a woman was a threat to me or my family."

"Well, you are in one now," said Plenty Hawk.

"In my lifetime, I have seen many women who are warriors," said Two Bears. "Among our people and among our enemies, I have never seen one more fierce in battle than a woman warrior."

"Well, I am sure women warriors are as brave and fierce as their male counterparts, but they are still women."

"Are you suggesting that we are weak, husband?" asked Mountain Flower.

"Absolutely not. I know women are a lot stronger than most of us men realize, it is just that..." He couldn't finish.

"You believe that as our husband, you are our protector," said Dark Wind.

"Yes. What example will I be setting for our son and all our future children that we will have, if I strike or kill a woman?"

Fighting Bear Woman gave her two cents. "I respect your principles, White Bear, but if any enemy is coming for you and your loved ones, then you must do whatever it takes to protect yourself and your family, even if the threat is a woman."

"And like my father said," said Dark Wind, "we are a lot stronger than you know."

"And we are still a family," added Mountain Flower. "We will face this danger together."

"Listen to your wives, White Bear," said Two Bears. "Sometimes, even a woman needs to protect her man."

"I agree," chuckled Plenty Hawk. "I mean, where would we be without women?"

"I can answer that," said Lazarus. "We would be dead!"

Everyone in the tipi laughed. "White Bear is wise beyond his years," said Two Bears.

"Marriage can do that," said Lazarus. "I guess it is settled then, whoever this new enemy is, we will face her together."

Both Dark Wind and Mountain Flower nodded and beamed with pride at their husband.

"Remember, my son," said Plenty Hawk. "You have friends who will fight to protect you."

"He is right, White Bear," added Lone Falcon. "Don't be afraid to call on us."

"I thank you," said Lazarus.

About a week later, near the Bighorn Mountains, Soaring Eagle Woman and her war party quietly came upon a Crow village near the Bighorn River, not far from the tributary of the Nowood River. They weren't sure if it was the village of Medicine Hawk, but it didn't matter. Their quarry was well known among the Crow. Broken Arrow recognized one of the Crow warriors riding out of the village.

"We are at the right Crow village," he signed. "That warrior riding out was among the defenders when we attacked them four moons ago."

"Then we shall follow him," said Soaring Eagle Woman. "When we capture him, I want him alive."

Lame Deer was a longtime friend of Lazarus Buchanan and his late Uncle Amos MacKinnon. As he was riding from the village to go hunting, he couldn't shake the feeling he was being watched. The forest was quiet, so someone or something was present. He knew it wasn't a grizzly bear because they were hibernating, and it wasn't a pack of wolves or a mountain lion because they would have attacked by now. Also, his horse wasn't skittish as it would be if it smelled those predators in close proximity.

Lame Deer was on edge. He was about two miles out from his village, so he stopped for a minute and continued to listen around him. The weather was cold, but it had stopped snowing the day before. As he looked down to see if there were any tracks, that's when they attacked. A Lakota warrior came out and threw his lance at Lame Deer's horse, striking the animal and causing it to fall. Lame Deer tried to go for his rifle, but it was too late. Another Lakota warrior stepped on his rifle to prevent him from lifting it. As he looked up, the warrior hit him with his war club and everything went black.

Soaring Eagle Woman appeared out of the forest, along with Spotted Cloud.

"Tie him up and put him on a horse," she said. "We will take him far from here, and when he wakes up, we make him talk."

Broken Arrow and the men tied up an unconscious Lame Deer and put him on one of their horses. They headed north, away from the village, without being spotted.

"What if he doesn't tell you what you want to know?" asked Spotted Cloud.

"I have ways of making an enemy talk," she said.

Spotted Cloud just smiled. "I'm sure you do."

10

TROUBLE IS COMING

SOARING Eagle Woman and her war party took their prisoner and traveled north up the Bighorn River, away from the Crow village. Once they were a safe distance away, they made a small camp. Lame Deer was now conscious, but he was gagged. He realized he had been taken by one of his people's greatest enemies, the Lakota. Why they took him, he didn't know, but he had a feeling he was about to find out. Some of the warriors went hunting, and while they were waiting for their return, Soaring Eagle Woman and Spotted Cloud approached their prisoner.

"We are going to cut your bonds," signed Spotted Cloud. "If you try to escape, you will die."

Lame Deer nodded his understanding. Spotted Cloud cut his bonds, allowing him to get circulation back in his wrists, so he could speak in sign.

"Now we have questions to ask you," signed Spotted Cloud. "Do you know a white man named White Bear?"

Lame Deer's expression immediately gave Soaring Eagle Woman and Spotted Cloud the answer. "He is my brother," signed Lame Deer. "Why do you hunt him?"

"He killed my brother," signed Soaring Eagle Woman.

Lame Deer looked around and noticed Broken Arrow. "I remember you," he signed and pointed to Broken Arrow. "You were part of a war party that attacked us a few moons ago."

Broken Arrow nodded. "I saw White Bear kill my friend River Fox," he signed. "He was Soaring Eagle Woman's brother."

Lame Deer turned his attention back to Soaring Eagle Woman. "White Bear is not a murderer," he said. "If he killed your brother, it was to protect our village and his family."

"Doesn't matter," she signed. "He still killed my brother and I will have my revenge."

"That doesn't explain why you captured me," said Lame Deer.

"You know where he lives," signed Soaring Eagle Woman. "He is your brother."

Lame Deer gave a defiant look. "I will never take you to where he lives. I will never betray White Bear."

"If you don't, you will die."

"Then I die."

Soaring Eagle Woman smirked. "As you wish." She took out her knife. "Any last words?" she signed.

"Tell White Bear's wives Dark Wind and Mountain Flower that Lame Deer said to kill you slow."

Spotted Cloud suddenly stopped Soaring Eagle Woman. "You said his wives," he signed. "Is one of them a Flathead?"

Lame Deer nodded. "The other is Nez Perce," he signed. "And they will fight to protect him, just as much as he would for them."

"Really?" said Soaring Eagle Woman.

"I will say no more," Lame Deer signed defiantly.

"I know everything I need to know," responded Soaring Eagle Woman. She stood behind him, grabbed his hair, and slit his throat. "I will take his body from here," she said. "Tomorrow we head for Flathead country."

Spotted Cloud sensed a change in the night air. "Another storm is coming," he said. "We should find shelter first and lay low until it passes."

Soaring Eagle Woman thought for a minute and agreed with the warrior. She dragged Lame Deer's body behind her horse about a mile away from camp and dumped it there, but not before taking his scalp.

Meanwhile, Lazarus and his family returned to their cabins in the Silver Bow Valley. It was decided that they would face this new enemy together. Trouble was coming and they knew it. Lazarus prayed to God it wouldn't cost him or his family their lives. Deep down, something was telling Lazarus that this enemy was coming for him and she was not going to wait until spring. In the frontier, you could never let your guard down. Lazarus knew this and he was not about to make that mistake. If anything, he thought it better to take the fight to the enemy.

He mentioned it to his wives and they thought it was a good idea, but they thought they should let the enemy come to them on their turf.

"This is our home," said Dark Wind. "We know this valley. The enemy, whoever she is, does not."

"And Chief Snake Killer and the Flatheads will help fight against this enemy," added Mountain Flower.

"I agree," said Lazarus. "I'm going to go hunting and see if I can snag up some game before the weather gets worse."

Meanwhile, back at the Crow village of Medicine Hawk, Hawk Eyes and Plain Feather were having dinner with her family when one of the warriors came riding in.

"Lame Deer's horse has been found," he said. Medicine Hawk left his tipi, followed by his wife Blue Willow, Plain Feather, and Hawk Eyes.

"What happened?" he asked.

"His horse looked like it was attacked by a lance," said the warrior. "Someone has taken him."

"Who?"

"I checked some of the tracks, and it looks like Lakota."

A surprised look appeared on Medicine Hawk's face. "They attack us again in the winter?"

"Why would they take Lame Deer?" asked Plain Feather.

"That's what I intend to find out," answered Medicine Hawk. "I will get a war party together and we will find him."

"A storm is coming, husband," said Blue Willow. "It looks like a bad a one."

"I will not stay in my lodge while one of my people has been taken by the enemy," responded Medicine Hawk.

"I will lead the war party, Uncle," said Running Dog. "You are needed here. Besides, Lame Deer is my friend."

Chief Medicine Hawk considered for a minute and thought that his nephew was right. "Find Lame Deer and bring him home, whether he is dead or alive," he said. "But be careful. Your aunt is right, this storm that is coming looks to be a bad one."

Running Dog nodded his understanding and got the war party together.

The storm came with a vengeance, but Soaring Eagle Woman and her warriors found shelter in a small cave. They managed to hunt down an elk and cut it into enough meat to feed the whole war party. The cave wasn't far above the ground. They could still reach their horses and there was enough grass around to feed the horses. However, the warriors managed to bring their animals close enough to the cave to prevent them from freezing. As the elk meat was cooking over the fire, some of the warriors wondered why the only enemy killed was the one Crow warrior they'd captured.

"We should have raided the village that Crow warrior was from," said one of the Lakota warriors.

"We were outnumbered," said Spotted Cloud. "To attack that village would have been folly."

"The enemy we hunt is worth ten scalps," said Soaring Eagle Woman. "Imagine the glory and medicine that will be heaped upon us if we capture him and bring him back alive?"

Most of the war party nodded their heads in agreement. Broken Arrow wasn't sure if this was a good idea, but he kept his opinions to himself. While the meat was still cooking, Soaring Eagle Woman went to the cave entrance and watched as the blizzard was raging.

"What are your thoughts?" asked Spotted Cloud as he walked up behind her.

"I pray that this blizzard dies soon."

"Patience," said Spotted Cloud. "Remember, a warrior has patience."

Soaring Eagle Woman nodded. "I will not let anyone stand in my way in capturing White Bear."

"I know," said Spotted Cloud. "Even kill his wives?"

"If I have to."

Spotted Cloud stood next to her, watching the storm. "I pray that this is not a mistake," he said. "Don't let vengeance consume you."

Soaring Eagle Woman nodded. She had great respect for Spotted Cloud, but it wasn't his brother that was killed by a *wasichu*, it was hers. She wanted vengeance, and she was going to get it no matter what may come.

11

A FIGHT IN THE STORM

As the storm died down a bit, Running Dog and his warriors were about a day's ride north from the village when they found Lame Deer's body. His throat was cut and his body was scalped. Running Dog screamed in despair over the death of his friend and brother.

"Who would do this?" asked Little Fox.

"I don't know," said Running Dog. "But I intend to find out and make the murderer pay!"

"It had to have been the Lakota," said Sky Hawk. He was the warrior who found Lame Deer's dead horse and he was known to be the best tracker in the village. "Their footprints were everywhere around his horse," he said.

"What doesn't make sense is why would they take Lame Deer this far out and kill him?" That was the question running through everyone's mind.

Running Dog looked up at the sky. He sensed that the weather was changing and the storm would die soon. "Little Fox, I want you to wrap Lame Deer's body in a buffalo robe and take it back to our village. Tell my uncle and Lame Deer's family that we found his body and we are going to head on to find his murderers as soon as the storm dies down."

"You can count on me, Running Dog," said Little Fox. Little Fox was only fifteen years old, but he was very mature and had proven himself in the eyes of the older warriors and elders. He considered it an honor that Running Dog entrusted him with the responsibility of taking his friend's body back to their village and reporting to Chief Medicine Hawk.

As the snowstorm died down a bit, Soaring Eagle Woman and her war party continued all the way up the Bighorn River to the Yellowstone River before heading west past Clark's Fork River. Some of the warriors grumbled, because despite the weather changing, it was still cold. However, the thought of capturing an enemy with strong medicine alive and bringing him back to their village to face justice was what moved them on to continue to follow their leader.

Soaring Eagle Woman was well respected among her people and there were very few men who challenged her. The only reason Broken Arrow agreed to accompany her and Spotted Cloud on this revenge raid was because River Fox was his friend. But, he was also afraid of Soaring Eagle Woman. She had proven on more than one occasion that she was not someone to be trifled with or underestimated. He had witnessed her brother fall in battle at the hands of this *wasichu* named White Bear. River Fox was just as fierce of a warrior as his sister, and to kill him in hand-to-hand combat would take someone of greater or equal skill.

Broken Arrow witnessed White Bear kill his friend in such a manner, and while he was not afraid of hunting him, he was cautious and feared that this could be a mistake. He would never tell Soaring Eagle Woman that, tough—at least not to her face.

It would take at least a week to reach the land of the Flatheads. The Lakota war party stealthily traveled through Three Forks, which was in Blackfeet country, in order to reach their destination. The weather changed often and it wasn't long before another snowstorm came. They stopped and camped at the Continental Divide. Spotted Cloud led some of the men to hunt, while Soaring Eagle Woman and Broken Arrow traveled on to scout ahead in the Silver Bow Valley. They were in no rush so they took their time due to the weather.

They traveled until nightfall, and when the weather cleared the next morning they continued on, until they came upon three cabins.

"What are those?" asked Broken Arrow.

"Wood lodges," answered Soaring Eagle Woman. "I have heard that *wasichu* trappers live in them all year round, but this is the first time I have seen one." Not far from the cabins was a corral fence surrounding at least a dozen horses. Suddenly, one of the cabin doors opened and a trapper appeared. He was big and tall and had white hair. From his advantage point, Broken Arrow immediately recognized him.

"That's him," he signed. "That is the *wasichu* who killed your brother."

Soaring Eagle Woman's blood began to boil, but she kept her anger in check. She'd promised her father that she would bring her brother's killer back alive if possible and that is what she intended to do.

"Let's go," she said.

"Where are we going?" asked Broken Arrow.

"To return to the others," said Soaring Eagle Woman. "We have found White Bear, and to capture him, we will need the others."

Lazarus Buchanan was enjoying the calm winter morning as he walked down to the corral to check on the horses. The weather was mild, but he knew another storm was coming soon. It was always like that here in the Rocky Mountains. Fortunately, the valley surrounding his home always protected him and his family from most of winter's wrath. Christmas was around the corner, and he had planned on going up into the high country to hunt bighorn sheep for the special occasion.

Suddenly, his sixth sense kicked in. Everything around the area became unnaturally quiet. Lazarus knew he was being watched. Dark Wind and Mountain Flower came out of the cabin with Little Amos and also sensed that something was wrong.

"We're being watched," said Lazarus.

"I know," said Dark Wind. "I can feel it, too."

Mountain Flower nodded in silent agreement.

"From now on, when we leave, we leave together," said Lazarus. "I am going to check the smokehouse to see if we need more meat." Both women nodded their understanding. Amos Winter Hawk wanted to go to his father and cried in protest when his mother picked him up and prevented him from doing so.

"Not now, little one," she said. "There is danger about."

"She is here," said Mountain Flower. "I feel it."

"So do I," responded Dark Wind. "We need to be ready."

A few days later, Soaring Eagle Woman and her war party were able to sneak into Silver Bow Valley before another blizzard hit. They managed to find shelter in the trees and kept out of sight, but even if they were able to capture their quarry the storm would prevent them from escaping. Instead, they kept watch on the cabins. When the opportunity arose, they would pounce and take White Bear.

That opportunity came on Christmas morning, when Lazarus and his family saddled up their horses to go hunt in the high country for bighorn sheep. Their sixth sense was still troubling them, however, they had been planning this trip for a while, so they were not about to cancel it. They remained fiercely cautious, though. As they were traveling in a northerly direction, Soaring Eagle Woman thought that it was time.

As Lazarus and his wives and infant son entered the forest, they quickly stopped as their sixth sense was blaring in alarm. The forest was quiet and they knew that they were in danger.

"We need to turn back," said Lazarus. Suddenly, two arrows hit the ground not far from the hooves of his horse. Mountain Flower was about to lift her rifle into a shooting position, but her husband stopped her. "Don't," he said. "If they wanted to kill us we would be dead already."

Before long, they found themselves surrounded by a group of Lakota warriors led by Soaring Eagle Woman herself. The warrior woman and Spotted Cloud approached, giving the peace sign. Lazarus responded in kind.

"You are the one called White Bear?" signed Soaring Eagle Woman.

"I am."

"We have come a long way to find you."

"Why?"

"You killed my brother!"

"You are Lakota?" Soaring Eagle Woman nodded. "When am I supposed to have committed this act?"

Broken Arrow rode up next to Soaring Eagle Woman. "In the land of the Crow," he signed. "We raided the Crow village of Medicine Hawk over four moons ago. You were there and defeated the brother of Soaring Eagle Woman in hand-to-hand combat."

Lazarus remembered. "I was defending my friends and family," he signed. "You would have done the same if we raided your village."

"True," said Soaring Eagle Woman. "Which is why if you surrender to us, your wives and son will not be harmed."

"You will not take our husband," signed Dark Wind. "You may kill us, but not before you join your brother!" Both women had their rifles in a ready to shoot position.

Spotted Cloud chuckled. He was impressed with the wives of White Bear. "Are you willing to die for this white man?" he asked in sign.

"We are," answered Mountain Flower.

"And I am willing to die for them," said Lazarus. "I have no quarrel with you or your people, but if you insist on going down this path of vengeance, I promise you that you will not take me alive, and you will be the first to die."

"So be it, White Bear!" signed Soaring Eagle Woman.

Suddenly, a gunshot rang out and Broken Arrow found a fatal bullet hole in his chest. The attack came from behind the war party as Running Dog and his Crow warriors charged. Without hesitation, both Dark Wind and Mountain Flower shot down two Lakota warriors, while their husband shot down another one that tried to club one of them. Soaring Eagle Woman, along with Spotted Cloud, quickly scattered when they realized they were outnumbered. They had not counted on the Crow to come and rescue White Bear and his family from their clutches.

The Lakota war party hastily took cover behind some fallen trees and rocks, while Lazarus and his family did the same in the opposite direction and quickly welcomed in their Crow friends as they boxed in their enemy. Soaring Eagle Woman and her warriors fought valiantly, but the odds had turned against them. Running Dog and his men, along with Lazarus and his wives, were cutting down the Lakota war party quickly.

Spotted Cloud suggested to Soaring Eagle Woman that they escape while they still had the chance. At first she refused. She wanted White Bear's scalp, but Spotted Cloud convinced her that now was not the time.

"We live to fight another day," he said. "Now we know where he lives and we will come back with more warriors."

Soaring Eagle Woman reluctantly gave in to the advice and signaled her surviving men to mount up and retreat. They managed to dodge arrows and bullets as they headed north then east out of the valley. Lazarus, Running Dog, and the rest of the Crow war party followed and chased them out of the valley, before returning triumphantly.

"How did you know?" asked Lazarus.

"Know what?" responded Running Dog.

"That my family and I were in danger and needed help."

"I didn't. Lame Deer's horse was found not far from our village and their tracks were surrounding the area, so we followed them to where they murdered him."

"Wait a minute," said a shocked Lazarus. "Lame Deer is dead?"

Running Dog sadly nodded. "His throat was cut and he was scalped."

Lazarus remembered seeing what looked like a Crow scalp hanging from Soaring Eagle Woman's belt. "It all makes sense now," he said.

"What do you mean?" asked Running Dog.

"The leader of that Lakota war party's name is Soaring Eagle Woman," said Lazarus. "I killed her brother when he and his warriors raided our village four moons ago. Now she wants vengeance."

Running Dog put two and two together. "Lame Deer knew where you and your family lived," he said. "She captured him in order to make him tell her."

"It is obvious that he didn't," said Lazarus. "I knew Lame Deer. He is dead because of me."

"This is not your fault, White Bear," said Running Dog. "This is her doing and hers alone."

Lazarus nodded. "It's not over," he said. "She now knows where I live and she will be back with more warriors."

"How can you be certain?"

"I killed her brother, Running Dog," said Lazarus. "It doesn't matter if it was in self-defense or not. I saw the fire in her eyes and she will not rest until I and everyone that I love is dead."

"What will you do, brother?" asked Running Dog.

"I'm taking my family over to Chief Snake Killer's village, where I know they will be safe. Then I will have to do what I must."

"That being?"

"Hunt that woman down and kill her before she kills me and anyone else that I care about!"

12

FIRST THINGS FIRST

AFTER THE BATTLE, the Lakota warriors that were killed were scalped and mutilated before their bodies were taken far from the land of White Bear to be left to the elements. Running Dog and his warriors were invited to stay with Lazarus and his family until the storm passed. Lazarus was going to take his wives and son to stay with the Flatheads before returning with Running Dog's men to Crow country to pay his respects to Lame Deer and find Soaring Eagle Woman.

He wasn't going to wait until spring. Dark Wind and Mountain Flower insisted on going with their husband, be he tried to convince them that he needed to do this alone. As usual, they would have none of it. They'd told him before and again that they were going to face this new threat to their family together, and now that they knew who she is, nothing was going to stop them from accompanying their husband to face the menace of this warrior woman.

Meanwhile, Soaring Eagle Woman and her surviving war party reached as far as Three Forks before another storm hit. They managed to find shelter and avoid any roving Blackfeet, who would gladly finish them off just for sport. Spotted Cloud was able to take down a mule deer and brought it to the small camp, where it was skinned, gutted, and cut up, then placed on the spit over the fire.

"So what do we do now?" asked one of the warriors.

"We return home," answered Soaring Eagle Woman. "For now."

"For now?" asked another warrior. "What do you mean for now?"

"I plan to return and capture or kill White Bear," said Soaring Eagle Woman. "Any warrior is welcome to join me, but those who stand in my way will regret it!"

"He has friends," said Gray Horn.

"Which is why we need more warriors," responded Spotted Cloud. The elder warrior looked at Gray Horn. "I noticed how you looked at White Bear's wives, Gray Horn," he said. "Would capturing them after we dispatch their husband influence you to join us in returning?"

The young Lakota warrior smirked. "They would make fine wives to warm my robes at night."

Soaring Eagle Woman humphed. "From what I saw, they would rather die first. We are definitely going to have to kill them, especially that Flathead bitch!"

"Well, will you at least let me have the Nez Perce or try to capture both of them after you kill their husband?" asked Gray Horn.

Soaring Eagle Woman just shrugged. "You're welcome to them, Gray Horn," she said. "But it is your scalp."

"First things first," said Spotted Cloud. "We must make it back home, tell your father what happened, and convince more warriors to join us."

Soaring Eagle Woman agreed without question.

"We may not have enough though," said Spotted Cloud. "When we return to your village, I will ride out to my village and convince my warriors to join our cause."

"What if they won't join us, Uncle?" asked Soaring Eagle Woman.

"They will," he said. "I can be very persuasive."

A couple of days later the storm died down. Lazarus, his wives, and the Crow war party went to the Flathead village of Chief Snake Killer. After paying their respects to the Chief and the council, they informed them what happened and let them know who the warrior woman was. While the Crow and the Flathead had not always been friends, on this day they were not enemies. Chief Snake Killer, Plenty Hawk, and the council thanked Running Dog and his friends for what they did for Lazarus, Dark Wind, and Mountain Flower.

"We have a common enemy," signed Running Dog. "And we have a common friend."

"Father," said Lazarus to Plenty Hawk. "We will not wait until spring for this Soaring Eagle Woman to return with a larger war party."

"I agree," said Plenty Hawk. "She now knows where you live, putting my daughters and grandson in grave danger."

While Mountain Flower was not related to Plenty Hawk and his wife by any means, she was honored that they treated and loved her like a daughter.

"You have my word that they will be safe with us as you go and face this new enemy," said Plenty Hawk.

"Mountain Flower and I are going with him father," said Dark Wind. Lazarus knew better than to argue with his wives and so did his father-in-law.

"A vengeance party is no place for a baby," said Plenty Hawk.

"I know, Father," said Dark Wind. "Which is why I wish for Winter Hawk to stay with you and mother."

Lone Falcon's wife Black Butterfly, who'd just had a baby a few months ago, volunteered to look after and breastfeed Lazarus and Dark Wind's baby. Even though the little tyke was almost two and growing teeth, he wasn't weaned yet. Lazarus and Dark Wind were grateful.

"We don't want you to go alone," said Chief Snake Killer. "The Lakota are our enemies also, so take as many warriors as you need."

"I will ride with my brother and sister to find and fight this new enemy," said Lone Falcon. A few more warriors also volunteered.

"Most of you are needed here," said Lazarus. "While I am honored that you are willing to join me, I can't and will not deprive the people of their protection."

Lazarus asked the council if Running Dog and his warriors could stay in the village for a couple of days, before they left to head east to their village. The council had no objections. After the council meeting was over, the medicine man Two Bears pulled Lazarus aside.

"White Bear," he said. "You are an honorable man who does not believe in making war on women, but you are also a husband and a father. This Soaring Eagle Woman intends to kill you and will stop at nothing to achieve her goal. You must do whatever it takes to protect yourself and your family!"

"I will, Uncle, and thank you," said Lazarus.

"May The Great Mystery protect you and those who follow you," said Two Bears.

"And you, too."

A few days later, the weather, while still cold, was okay enough to travel in. Lazarus, Dark Wind, Mountain Flower, and a coalition of Flathead and Crow warriors left the village and traveled east to the Bighorn River. They headed south, avoiding Three Forks, before heading east, following the Shoshone River. It took them a week to reach the Crow village of Chief Medicine Hawk, but they made it to the Bighorn River.

It was now the second week of January in the year of our Lord 1815. Lazarus was now twenty-one, but he was in no mood to celebrate his birthday. First things first after greeting his late uncle's widow Plain Feather, her husband Hawk Eyes, and his little cousin Angus White Cloud and the rest of the family, Lazarus wanted to pay his respects to Lame Deer's family. Lame Deer's parents, Red Fox and Singing Grass, welcomed Lazarus into their lodge. As a sign of mourning their hair had been cut, so Lazarus, who was a good friend of their son, did the same and had his wives cut their hair as well. Red Fox and Singing Grass appreciated this.

"Red Fox," said Lazarus. "It is my fault that your son is dead."

"How so?"

"The Lakota woman who killed him wanted information from him," said Lazarus. "She wanted him to tell her where I lived, but I believe he died because he refused to tell her." Tears were streaming down Lazarus' cheeks.

Singing Grass approached him and placed her hands on his

shoulders. "My son died as he lived," she said. "With honor and loyalty for those that he cared about and loved."

"This is not your fault, White Bear," added Red Fox. "You did not kill my son, this Lakota woman did."

"She will pay," said Lazarus. "I promise you, I will avenge your son or die in the attempt."

"My son was not a man of vengeance, White Bear," said Singing Grass. "He would not want you or anyone to live for one moment in vengeance, not even for him!" Her statement gave him pause.

"If you let vengeance consume you, White Bear," said Red Fox, "then you are no different than the woman who took my son."

"They are right, Lazarus," said Plain Feather. "Is that what you want? Is that what your Uncle would have wanted?"

"No," answered Lazarus. "It no longer matters what I want, though."

"Why?"

"Because Soaring Eagle Woman will not stop until I am dead. I have to kill her before she kills me or worse."

"And what would be worse than her killing you?" asked Hawk Eyes.

"Any more of you getting hurt or killed in the middle of this," answered Lazarus. "I have already lost an Uncle, now I have lost a friend. I'm not going to lose any more people that I love dearly, not if I can help it!"

13

THERE WILL BE BLOOD

ANOTHER STORM HAD COME to the Bighorn Mountains. While Lazarus and some of his friends from both the Crow and Flathead were anxious to be on the move, the elders and their families strongly advised against traveling east to Lakota country in such weather.

"If it is dangerous to hunt down Soaring Eagle Woman in such weather, then it is dangerous for her to hunt you or any of us also," said Chief Medicine Hawk.

The advice was sound and they took it. When the weather did permit, Lazarus, Running Dog, Lone Falcon, Hawk Eyes, and some other warriors would go hunting. Little did they know, however, that Soaring Eagle Woman had left two spies behind to watch over the village of Medicine Hawk. These two men, who were with the original war party that tried to capture Lazarus at his home, volunteered to stay behind and keep watch in case he came to visit his Crow friends. Hawk Eyes sensed that the hunting party was being watched, so he casually separated from the group and went to investigate the surrounding area.

"Why did we volunteer to stay behind?" asked Yellow Horse.

Gray Horn just looked at his friend in contempt. "White Bear has friends," he said. "If we are going to successfully capture him, we can't have a repeat of the Crow or any of his friends coming to his aid."

"Well, it appears that we won't have to try and capture him," said Yellow Horse. "Since he and his women arrived with a contingent of both Crow and Flathead a couple of sleeps ago, it looks like they are not going to wait for us to come to them."

Gray Horn had come to the same conclusion. "When the weather changes we ride back to Soaring Eagle Woman to tell her."

Out of nowhere, an arrow struck the ground between the two Lakota spies. Yellow Horse was about to go for his lance, but Gray Horn warned him against it. Hawk Eyes appeared from the bushes. He quickly replaced his bow and arrow with his two pistols, covering the duo.

"Nez Perce dog!" shouted Yellow Horse in Lakota.

Hawk Eyes didn't understand his words, but he knew he had just been insulted. Without hesitation, he shot Yellow Horse right between the eyes with one of his pistols. He kept the remaining loaded one on Gray Horn, shaking his head, warning him to stay still. The gunshot was heard and it wasn't long before the hunting party arrived.

"It appears we have spies," said Running Dog in Crow.

"It appears so," added Lazarus. After they dismounted, Lazarus recognized Gray Horn, who looked at him with defiant eyes. "Take your friend and ride back to Soaring Eagle Woman with a message," signed Lazarus. "You tell her that I am coming. If she wants peace, then I will accept it, but if she wants war then there will be blood and it will be either hers or mine."

"She will never offer you peace," signed Gray Horn. "Nor will she accept it." Gray Horn wrapped Yellow Horse's body in a buffalo robe and tied it to his horse. He was allowed to mount his horse, but before he rode away, he gave one last message. "When we meet next time in battle, White Bear, the scalp of your Nez Perce brother will hang from my belt and your women will be mine," he signed.

"Pray that we don't meet again then," signed Lazarus.

"I accept your challenge," signed Hawk Eyes.

Gray Horn rode out of Crow Country as fast as he could.

"We shouldn't have let him go," said Running Dog.

"Perhaps," said Lazarus. "But I want Soaring Eagle Woman to know that I am coming and I will not live in fear, not from her or from any enemy!" Lazarus looked up in the sky to get a gauge on the weather. "We best get back to hunting while we still can," he said. "In a few sleeps more, we ride to Lakota country."

A couple of days later, Gray Horn arrived at his village with Yellow Horse's body. He gave Lazarus' message to Soaring Eagle Woman, letting her know that her prey was coming.

"This is good," she said.

"It is the middle of winter," said Black Bull. "To make war now holds no advantage for him or us."

"White Bear has proven to be no fool," said Soaring Eagle Woman. "He knows that I will not rest until I have his scalp hanging from my belt, or mine hanging from his. He will not wait until the spring. He wants to finish this now, once and for all."

"What will you do, Daughter?" asked Chief Wolf Killer.

"I'm going to help White Bear find me," answered Soaring Eagle Woman. "*I* will be the one to end this once and for all."

"You should wait for Spotted Cloud," said Black Bull. "He will be here in a few sleeps. Besides, it is too dangerous to travel back west with the way the weather is."

"Black Bull is right," said Chief Wolf Killer. "If White Bear is no fool, then he knows this as well. He is probably in no hurry himself."

"How can you be so sure, Father?"

"Remember, my child, a warrior never underestimates the enemy," answered Chief Wolf Killer. "Let White Bear and his friends come to us. At least that way, we can fight him on our ground and on our terms."

Soaring Eagle Woman listened to the advice of her father and uncle. It made sense.

"Alright," she said. "We will wait for Spotted Cloud and when the weather changes for the better."

The elders nodded their heads in agreement. "You will make a fine Chief one day, Soaring Eagle Woman," said Black Bull.

"You honor me, Uncle," she said. "But until I deserve that honor, I will not rest until I have White Bear's head."

Lazarus, Dark Wind, Mountain Flower, Plain Feather, Hawk Eyes, Running Dog, Lame Deer, and the war party contingent of both Crow and Flatheads left the village of Chief Medicine Hawk a few days after catching the Lakota spies. It was still the middle of January, but the winter weather was mild. There was still snow on the ground, but at least the blizzard was finally gone. Lazarus prayed that another one would not come, but in the Rocky Mountains during the winter, the weather was far from predictable. So far, the mild weather had made traveling agreeable.

The war party headed east, crossing the Powder River into the eastern plains of modern day Wyoming. They camped at the southern edge of the Belle Fourche River, where the leaders started to get a plan together.

"Soaring Eagle Woman and her warriors know we are coming," said Lazarus.

"I agree," said Lone Falcon. "If I was them I would plan an ambush."

"It makes sense," said Hawk Eyes. "We will be fighting in their country on their turf." It was quiet for a moment.

"We should send scouts ahead," said Running Dog.

"I agree," said Lazarus. "I will scout ahead and see what we are up against."

"You're not going alone," said Dark Wind.

"You two ladies are not coming with me," said Lazarus. "I want you to stay here in case something goes wrong."

"We have already discussed this, husband," said Mountain Flower.

"I know, but if anything happened to any of you, I would never forgive myself."

"I will go with him," volunteered Plain Feather. "I have been to the Lakota Country and around the Belle Fourche River." Lazarus was about to object, but a look from his aunt told him that it would be a losing battle.

"I don't suppose I can talk you out of it?"

"You have a better chance of capturing the wind, nephew," said Plain Feather.

"I guess that settles it then," said Lazarus. "We leave at sunset."

"Be careful, you two," said Running Dog.

"We will, cousin," responded Plain Feather.

14

CAPTURED

THE BELLE FOURCHE RIVER is a tributary of the Cheyenne River. It is exactly 290 miles long and covers what is now the states of Wyoming and South Dakota. Lazarus Buchanan and Plain Feather left the camp as soon as the sun set, following the Belle Fourche River heading east. They traveled cautiously, hoping to avoid not just Soaring Eagle Woman's people, but also their allies the Cheyenne and Arapaho, who often frequented the area. While grizzly and black bears, along with rattlesnakes were still hibernating for the winter, Lazarus and his aunt had to worry about packs of hungry wolves, mountain lions, and wolverines. This was the price that many trappers paid while living on the frontier.

American Indians had been living with Mother Nature and its dangers since the beginning of time. They were used to it, because it was the way of things. Lazarus Buchanan did not want to kill Soaring Eagle Woman, just like he had not wanted to kill her brother, but he was left with no choice. Lazarus was a man of peace and preferred to live in peace with anyone who chose to live in peace with him. But he would not hesitate to remove a threat to him or his family and friends and would fight and kill that threat with the furor of an angry she-grizzly protecting her cubs.

They continued to travel, following the river but staying close to the trees so they wouldn't be seen. There was no need to hunt because Lazarus and his Aunt Plain Feather had packed enough pemmican to sustain them for a while. Plus, Plain Feather was an expert at finding edible plant roots that grew throughout the winter. They were about ten miles from their war party as they settled down to lay low for the day.

"We shouldn't be far from the Bear Lodge Mountains," said Plain Feather. Lazarus just nodded. "You're awfully quiet. nephew."

"Just got a lot on my mind," said Lazarus. "All this killing ain't necessary."

"I agree," said Plain Feather. "But it is the way of things, and Soaring Eagle Woman has given you no choice."

"You really believe there is no chance of her accepting peace?"

Plain Feather shook her head. "From what I have heard about her, she is a great and fierce warrior," she said. "A credit to her people, surely, but she has a heart of stone."

Lazarus just sighed. Then thoughts of his late Uncle Amos appeared. Plain Feather was reading his mind. "I miss him, too, nephew," she said. "More than you know."

"I believe he would have been proud of you and White Cloud," said Lazarus.

"He would have been proud of you as well," responded Plain Feather.

Suddenly, he heard a noise from the east of their camp. It sounded like a stampede of horses. Lazarus immediately put the fire out, before he and Plain Feather went to investigate. As they went for their horses, a Lakota warrior on horseback appeared out of the forest. He looked just as surprised to see them as they were to see him. After overcoming his initial shock, the warrior attempted to throw his lance, however, Lazarus quickly fired his Pennsylvania rifle, knocking the warrior off his horse.

"Ride to the others," he shouted to his aunt. "I will draw the rest of them away from you to give you time to escape!"

"I'm not leaving you," said Plain Feather. More Lakota warriors were heading in their direction, and there was no time to argue.

"The hell you ain't!" Lazarus kicked Plain Feather's horse in the rump, causing it to head in the westerly direction, carrying her with it. Lazarus managed to mount his horse just as the Lakota war party arrived. "Come and get me, you bastards!" he shouted, before riding north.

"That's him!" said Gray Horn. "That's White Bear! After him!"

Without hesitation, the Lakota war party of about thirty warriors chased after Lazarus, giving Plain Feather a chance to escape.

Plain Feather rode as fast as her horse could carry her. She was at least ten miles from her friends and family and she prayed the weather would remain agreeable enough for her to reach them and come back and rescue Lazarus before it was too late.

Meanwhile, Lazarus had managed to lure the Lakota away from Plain Feather, but he made a miscalculation and boxed himself into a small canyon with no way out. He didn't have time to reload his Pennsylvania rifle, but he did still have his loaded pistols and knife, but he knew that there was no chance of him winning a fight against a war party that outnumbered him thirty-to-one. He quickly turned his horse around and faced his enemies. The Lakota war party led by Gray Horn surrounded the trapper.

"Remember," said Gray Horn in Lakota, "Soaring Eagle Woman wants him alive."

Lazarus raised his empty rifle in the air with both hands as a sign of surrender. Gray Horn had his warriors immediately disarm him. After that was done, he approached him.

"We meet again, White Bear," he signed. Lazarus just nodded. "Where are your people?"

"I am alone," answered Lazarus. "You lie," signed Gray Horn. "Even you wouldn't be so foolish to come after Soaring Eagle Woman all by yourself in our own land!"

Lazarus just smirked. Something was amiss and the Lakota warrior knew it. "Tie him," he commanded. "We take him back to Soaring Eagle Woman!"

Suddenly, two other warriors arrived. They spoke to Gray Horn at length in Lakota, before he turned his attention back to the prisoner. "Where is the Crow woman who was with you?" he signed. Lazarus defiantly remained silent. "It doesn't matter now," said Gray Horn. "We take him back to the village!"

The village of Chief Wolf Killer was not far from where Lazarus was captured. Gray Horn and his men immediately brought Lazarus to Soaring Eagle Woman and her father. The body of the Lakota warrior that Lazarus had shot and killed was brought in to his family and as a result, everyone's bloodlust was up.

"So this is the *wasichu* who killed my son?" asked Chief Wolf Killer.

"Yes, Father," answered Soaring Eagle Woman.

"We have reason to believe that he is not alone," said Gray Horn. "With his dying breath, White Rabbit said he caught him with a Crow woman."

"Does he know sign?" asked Chief Wolf Killer.

"He does, Father," answered Soaring Eagle Woman.

"Untie him," ordered Chief Wolf Killer. One of the warriors untied Lazarus. After rubbing his wrists together, the trapper gave his captors his undivided attention. "Where are your people, White Bear?" Chief Wolf Killer signed. "I suggest you speak with a straight tongue."

"It does not matter if I speak with a straight tongue or not," signed Lazarus. "You will kill me anyway for the life of your son."

"This is true."

"I want you to know, like I told your daughter, I did not want to kill your son, but he was trying to kill me."

Chief Wolf Killer nodded his understanding. "And White Rabbit?" he said, pointing to the body of the Lakota Lazarus had killed. "Did he leave you no choice as well?"

Lazarus nodded. "He tried to kill me with his lance."

"Why are you in our land. White Bear?"

"Because your daughter hunts me," answered Lazarus. "She

intends to kill me at any cost, even if that means threatening my family, and I can't allow that."

Soaring Eagle Woman gave a smirk. "The Crow woman that was with you," she signed. "Who is she to you?"

"She is my Uncle's widow," answered Lazarus.

"And where is she?"

A look of defiance appeared on Lazarus' face. "I will say no more," he said.

Chief Wolf Killer and some of the members on the council appeared to be impressed by Lazarus Buchanan. It appeared that he was willing to die for those he cared about, which was something they themselves would do.

"You appear to be an honorable man, White Bear," said Chief Wolf Killer. "But it doesn't change the fact that you have killed my son and now another member of my people."

"I am sorry for that," said Lazarus. "I really am sorry."

Suddenly Spotted Cloud, along with Black Bull appeared out of the crowd. He asked Chief Wolf Killer permission to speak to the prisoner. The Chief granted it.

"You said the Crow woman was your Uncle's widow?" asked Spotted Cloud. Lazarus nodded. "Did your uncle have white hair like you?"

A look of surprise appeared on Lazarus' face. "How did you know?" he asked.

Spotted Cloud smiled. "We have met before in battle," he answered. "Almost five summers ago in the land of the Omaha."

"Enough of this!" shouted Soaring Eagle Woman. "This *wasichu* must die and he must die now!"

"Patience, my daughter," said Chief Wolf Killer. "That is a decision for the council." Chief Wolf Killer had Lazarus bound and taken to one of the lodges, where he would be kept until the council decided his fate.

Little did anyone in the village know, Plain Feather not only made it back to her friends and family among the war party, but they managed to track Lazarus and his captors back to the Lakota village.

Dark Wind had Lazarus' spyglass and was able to see where the Lakota were keeping him. She, along with everyone else, were truly grateful he was still alive, but they knew unless something was done soon he wouldn't be alive for long. Once they saw where Lazarus was kept, Mountain Flower and Hawk Eyes volunteered to sneak into the village and rescue him. No one objected.

Later that evening, the council decided that Lazarus would die by torture at the next sunrise. Soaring Eagle Woman and her father relayed the news to their prisoner. Lazarus remained stoic as he was told of his impending demise. He was allowed to have his hands free in order to speak in sign.

"Vengeance will not give you peace, Soaring Eagle Woman," he said. "Trust me, I know."

"How can you know, white dog?"

"Because I lost my Uncle to a Blackfoot warrior," responded Lazarus. "He was more like a father to me than an uncle and I killed that Blackfoot warrior for what he took from me."

"Then you have balanced the scale," said Chief Wolf Killer.

"Have I?" asked Lazarus. "My Uncle is still dead, his son no longer has a father, his wife no longer has a husband." Both Chief Wolf Killer and his daughter were impressed. But only a little bit.

"If only you were an Oglala," said Soaring Eagle Woman, "I might have considered taking you as my husband."

"I thank the Creator that I was born as I am," responded Lazarus. "I don't blame you for not trusting the white man. We have done nothing to earn that trust, but I am not sorry for being born white."

"Nor should you be," said Chief Wolf Killer. Soaring Eagle Woman just huffed and stormed out of the lodge.

"Again, I am truly sorry for taking your son's life," said Lazarus. "I wish there could have been another way."

"As do I," responded Chief Wolf Killer.

Lazarus' hands were retied by the guards before Chief Wolf Killer left.

As the moon reached its zenith, Mountain Flower and Hawk Eyes snuck through the horse herd and slipped into the village. The lodge where Lazarus was kept was near the herd by the river. Mountain Flower and Hawk Eyes managed to cut through the lodge opposite of the entrance and sneak in. Lazarus was wide awake; he couldn't sleep. He smiled when he saw his wife and his friend come in. No words were said as Mountain Flower immediately cut the ropes that bound her husband's hands and feet. When the coast was clear, the trio made it out the back, through the horse herd.

When one of the horse guards spotted them, he was about to sound the alarm, but Dark Wind's arrow silenced him. She had snuck in and stayed by the herd while Hawk Eyes and Mountain Flower went to rescue Lazarus. Dark Wind led them down the trail by the river and back to their people who were waiting for them. They were at least a mile out from the village and hidden in the forest, near the Bear Lodge Mountains.

"To say that I am happy to see all of you is an understatement," said Lazarus.

"The Great Mystery smiles on you, my brother," said Running Dog. "So what happens next?"

"At sunrise, we attack," answered Lazarus. "I want to finish this once and for all."

15

THE BATTLE OF BELLE FOURCHE RIVER

THE VERY NEXT MORNING, Soaring Eagle Woman, Spotted Cloud, Chief Wolf Killer, and Black Bull went to the lodge to retrieve Lazarus. The guards went inside only to find that he was gone. They saw that the back of the lodge wall was cut and that someone had snuck in and helped Lazarus escape. Suddenly, a cry was heard from the horse herd and the village, led by Chief Wolf Killer, rushed to investigate. The body of one of the herd guards was found with what appeared to be a Flathead arrow to his throat.

"Whoever came for White Bear and helped him escape, they couldn't have gone far," said Soaring Eagle Woman.

"They haven't," responded Spotted Cloud. "Look yonder!"

Not far from the village, on the western horizon, over a hundred Crow and Flathead warriors appeared, facing the village. They were painted for war and in the lead were Running Dog, Lone Falcon, Lazarus Buchanan, Hawk Eyes, Plain Feather, Dark Wind, and Mountain Flower.

Lazarus was carrying a Flathead lance with a white flag tied to it. He instructed his friends not to fire without his say-so. He wanted to give peace a final chance with a parley. He slowly approached the village, stopping halfway. Chief Wolf Killer, Soaring Eagle Woman, and Spotted Cloud mounted their horses and rode out to meet him.

"Well done, White Bear," signed Spotted Cloud. "You have escaped our grasp once again."

"There does not need to be any more bloodshed," responded Lazarus. "I want to be left in peace. Give me your word, Soaring Eagle Woman, that you will leave me and my family and friends alone and we will not attack."

"It is too late for that, White Bear," signed Soaring Eagle Woman. "You will never know peace while I am alive. I will take your scalp, just like I took your Crow friend's." Soaring Eagle Woman raised the scalp of Lame Deer in front of Lazarus, causing the trapper to turn blood red.

"I will see you on the field of battle," he signed. Lazarus quickly turned his horse around and rode back to his people, while Chief Wolf Killer, Soaring Eagle Woman, and Spotted Cloud did the same. While they and the Lakota warriors prepared for battle, the women, children, and elderly fled for safety near the trees.

Lazarus nodded his head to Running Dog and Lone Falcon and both men gave the war cry. They were followed by the contingent of their Crow and Flathead brethren, before they charged straight for the village. Soaring Eagle Woman led her Lakota warriors out to greet the oncoming war party and the two groups crashed right into each other. Gray Horn still had Lazarus' weapons, so Lazarus was armed with only a knife and a war club he'd borrowed from Lone Falcon. It was enough, for the trapper managed to take down two Lakota warriors with the war club, before dodging a bullet fired from his own rifle. Gray Horn didn't have time to reload, so he tried to go for Lazarus pistols, but the trapper was on him quick, clubbing him with the war club, and while the Lakota warrior was down, Lazarus managed to stab him twice with the knife.

Soaring Eagle Woman saw him and was about to attack from behind, but her horse was shot out from under her and it collapsed, trapping her leg under its side. Spotted Cloud was nearby and managed to reach her through the melee and pull her out. As they were both standing, they saw Dark Wind and Mountain Flower, standing opposite them, pointing a pistol each at them.

"My fight is with White Bear," signed Soaring Eagle Woman. "Not you two."

"Then your fight *is* with us," responded Dark Wind.

"We will not let you kill our husband," added Mountain Flower.

Spotted Cloud gave a look of admiration towards the two wives of White Bear, before taking out his tomahawk and charging. Both women fired simultaneously at point blank range. With two new holes in his chest, Spotted Cloud fell to his knees, singing his death song. Soaring Eagle Woman, realizing that the women's pistols were now empty, charged with her tomahawk, but was quickly shot in the shoulder, courtesy of Plain Feather's rifle. The force of the bullet strike knocked her down, and when she realized that she had been wounded, she looked at the Crow woman.

Plain Feather, who had been fighting at Hawk Eyes' side, managed to reload and gave a look of warning to the Lakota woman. Dark Wind and Mountain Flower had managed to reload their pistols and they were finally joined by their husband. The battle had turned in their favor, as the Lakota warriors were being cut down and defeated. Seeing the writing on the wall, Soaring Eagle Woman managed to get up and mount a riderless horse and head back to the village.

After retrieving his weapons, Lazarus mounted his horse to chase after Soaring Eagle Woman. "This is not over," he said to his wives. "This ends today!" Lazarus kicked his horse's sides and charged after his enemy. Little did he know that his wives and his aunt were not going to let him go alone. All three women managed to mount their horses and follow Lazarus. No matter what, this was going to end— with either Soaring Eagle Woman dying or them.

Soaring Eagle Woman rode past her village towards the Belle Fourche River with Lazarus hot on her tail. She managed to cross the shallow part of the river, over to the other side. She was trying to head southeast to the badlands, but she realized too late that her horse was lame. She stopped for a minute to check her shoulder wound. The bullet didn't appear to have hit any bone or vitals, but it needed tending or it could get infected. However, she knew that if White Bear was chasing her, none of that would matter. She would face her enemy, one way or another.

She got her wish when Lazarus Buchanan appeared.

With a look of defiance, Soaring Eagle Woman dismounted, took out her knife, and issued an open challenge to Lazarus.

He just shook his head. "It doesn't have to end this way," he signed.

"This is the only way it ends, White Bear!"

Lazarus looked at the scalp of his friend Lame Deer, hanging from Soaring Eagle Woman's belt. He immediately pulled his pistol and aimed, but he couldn't pull the trigger. Killing a woman was against everything he believed in.

"I will not kill you," he signed. "I will not strike down a woman."

"Then you are a fool," she signed back. Soaring Eagle Woman gave out a defiant war cry and charged. She didn't get very far, when three gunshots rang out, cutting her down. She fell dead at the hooves of Lazarus' horse. Lazarus turned around to see where the gunshots came from. Not far from him, stood his wives and his Aunt Plain Feather, all carrying smoking rifles. He nodded his thanks before he dismounted.

As he turned Soaring Eagle Woman over, it was clear she was dead. Her eyes were open, but they no longer saw the world of the living. Lazarus closed them and retrieved Lame Deer's scalp from her belt. The women approached and dismounted.

"Are you going to take her scalp, husband?" asked Dark Wind.

"No," he said. "But I will return her body to her people. She deserves a burial fitting a warrior."

"I agree," said Plain Feather. "Do not feel sad, nephew. You gave her every chance."

"She is right, husband," said Mountain Flower. "Soaring Eagle Woman would have never accepted peace."

"A woman with a heart of stone never does," added Dark Wind.

"Thank you," said Lazarus. "All three of you."

"For what?" asked Dark Wind.

"For saving my life."

"We are family, nephew," said Plain Feather. "You never have to thank us for that."

16

ENOUGH BLOOD HAS BEEN SHED

THE BATTLE between the Lakota and the coalition of Flathead and Crow warriors had ended. Running Dog and Lone Falcon's people won, defeating Chief Wolf Killer and his Lakota warriors as they retreated towards the forest. They made one last stand to protect the women, children, and the elderly, but the Flathead and Crow did not pursue. Lazarus, Dark Wind, Mountain Flower, and Plain Feather returned with the body of Soaring Eagle Woman. They stopped near the empty village, before Lazarus, under a flag of truce, rode out toward the Lakota to return Soaring Eagle Woman's body.

"Chief Wolf Killer," he signed. "I come in peace and wish to speak to you." Chief Wolf Killer and Black Bull rode out of the trees to meet with Lazarus. "I return your daughter's body to you," he signed.

A look of sadness was on the Lakota Chief's face, but he was surprised. "Did you scalp her?"

Lazarus shook his head. "I didn't even kill her," he said. "My wives and my aunt did."

This surprised both Chief Wolf Killer and Black Bull. "You didn't kill her nor cut up her body?" asked Black Bull.

"That is not my way," answered Lazarus. "I don't make war on women and children, and my wives and my aunt only did what they had to do."

Wolf Killer and Black Bull looked at each other, before returning their gaze back to the trapper. "So what happens next?" asked Chief Wolf Killer.

"That depends," answered Lazarus. "Is this finished?"

Chief Wolf Killer sighed and looked up in the sky. The weather was still cold, but mild. Everyone sensed that it would change and that another winter storm was coming.

"Go in peace, White Bear," he finally said. "Enough blood has been shed." Lazarus nodded and handed the reins of the horse carrying Soaring Eagle Woman's body to her father.

Lazarus returned to his wives, aunt, and friends and told them that it was over. "It is time to go home," he said. No one objected.

"Soaring Eagle Woman and her people?" asked Running Dog.

"She is dead," answered Plain Feather.

"And as far as her people are concerned," added Lazarus, "we need not worry about them. Enough blood has been shed. On that, we have agreed."

"This is good," said Running Dog. "We best hurry, another storm is coming."

"I agree," said Lazarus. "I almost forgot." Lazarus handed Running Dog Lame Deer's scalp.

The Crow warrior's eyes began to water as he thanked his friend for retrieving it. "Now my brother can go to the Happy Hunting Grounds in peace," he said.

They immediately left the Belle Fourche River, heading west back toward the Bighorn River. It took a couple of days to return to the village of Chief Medicine Hawk, but they made it without incident. By the time they arrived, the winter storm hit the Bighorn Mountains with a fury. This bothered Lazarus and Dark Wind, mainly because they were anxious to get back to the Flathead, where their son was. However, Lone Falcon assured his sister that the baby was safe with his aunt and grandparents. The storm, no matter how long it lasted, was just a delay.

As they got settled in, the Crow and their Flathead friends paid their respects to Lame Deer's family and returned his scalp to them. Despite the weather, Lame Deer's parents, followed by the village, went to his funeral scaffold and his mother reattached his scalp to his head to the best of her ability. Lazarus said a silent prayer to God, for his friend and for all the lives lost in the battle that took place a few days before. He prayed not just for his friends, but also for the Lakota who died that day. Following his Presbyterian upbringing, Lazarus did not take joy in the suffering of his enemies or their death. He hated fighting, but did what he must to protect the ones he loved. As he silently prayed, he thanked God for his wives and his aunt Plain Feather. While they may be stubborn, he wouldn't be alive if they were otherwise. and he knew it and was grateful for it.

After the funeral of Lame Deer, a feast was held and the story of the battle with the Lakota was told. Since Dark Wind, Mountain Flower, and Plain Feather killed Soaring Eagle Woman, they were asked to tell the village about it. The women were not braggarts and explained that killing the woman, who sought the life of the man that they all loved dearly, was nothing. Lazarus didn't disagree.

"My aunt and my wives did what I could not," he said in Crow and in Flathead. "Many of you know that I don't believe in making war against women and children, and that I would never strike down a woman." Everyone listened intently. Some were very curious about Lazarus and his principles. "Which is why I am grateful to the Creator for my wives and my aunt," he continued. "If it wasn't for them, I would be dead by now. They have proven to be as fierce as any warrior and just as much as they are proud of me, I am even more proud of them!"

With that, Chief Medicine Hawk and the entire village whooped and cheered in praise for Dark Wind, Mountain Flower, and Plain Feather. Little Angus White Cloud ran to his mother and hugged her, giving a little imitation of a war cry and a whoop. Lazarus looked at his two-and-a-half-year-old cousin. A tear ran down his cheek as he saw so much of his Uncle Amos in him.

"He looks like his father," said Hawk Eyes. "Doesn't he?"

"He does," answered Lazarus. "Wait a minute, how do you know what his father looks like?"

Hawk Eyes gave his nephew a smirk. "Well, he doesn't look like me," he said. "Who else is he supposed to look like, other than his mother?"

For the first time Lazarus laughed. "That is true," he said. "I hope this storm lets up soon. I want to get back home as soon as possible and be reunited with my son."

"Patience, husband," said Dark Wind. "Our son is in good hands and we will be reunited with him soon." Dark Wind looked at Mountain Flower and winked. "In the meantime," she said, "Mountain Flower needs you."

At first Lazarus had a look of confusion, then Dark Wind whispered in his ear, causing him to turn beet red. He took Mountain Flower by the hand and they walked outside towards their lodge. It was going to be a long, pleasurable night.

17

SPRING TRAPPING SEASON

THE WINTER STORM lasted a couple of days. Once it cleared, Lazarus, Dark Wind, Mountain Flower, Plain Feather, Hawk Eyes, and the Flathead warriors were ready to be on the move and return home to Flathead country. It was near the end of January and the weather was once again mild and agreeable for travel. They said their goodbyes to friends and family, leaving the village of Chief Medicine Hawk. They followed the Shoshone River into what is now Yellowstone National Park. While traveling through there, Lazarus couldn't help but be in awe at what he saw. He remembered John Colter telling him and his uncle about the geysers and the boiling pots as well as the great waterfalls that took your breath away. Even in the winter, the boiling pots raised the temperatures around them and the group saw some buffalo bathing in the warm water nearby. They continued to travel, not letting their guard down for a second as they stared in wonder at the beautiful surroundings.

A couple of days later they made it home in the Silver Bow Valley. As was the custom, the women checked the cabins to see that they didn't have any unwanted visitors in residence, while Lazarus, Hawk Eyes, and the rest of the warriors went to corral the horses. The only visitors to their home were rodents, but they quickly dispersed when chased out of the cabins.

The smokehouse needed meat, so Lazarus and some of the warriors planned to do some hunting before finding the village of Chief Snake Killer. However, Lone Falcon and two of his warriors volunteered to head out to find his people and promised to return with his family, including Lazarus and Dark Wind's baby boy Amos Winter Hawk, who was now two years old.

A few days later, Lone Falcon returned with his wife Black Butterfly, his parents Plenty Hawk and Fighting Bear Woman, and both his son Panther and his nephew Amos Winter Hawk. To say that Lazarus, Dark Wind, and Mountain Flower were overjoyed to be reunited with their baby boy would be an understatement.

It took a while for the little tyke to recognize his parents, but before long, he was smiling and jumping on his father's lap and was already talking, saying mama and dada in both English and Flathead. The village as usual was not far from where Lazarus and his family lived, so the warriors stayed for a few more days before heading home. Dark Wind's parents informed Lazarus that everyone in the village was doing well, and while the winter was still difficult, they were managing.

The next day, Lazarus, Plenty Hawk, Hawk Eyes, and Lone Falcon went hunting to provide for their families and restock the smokehouse. They split up in twos, and both duos were successful. Lazarus and Plenty Hawk took a full-grown bull moose, while Hawk Eyes and Lone Falcon took down a full-grown bull elk, a mere couple of miles from their homestead. Lone Falcon and Plenty Hawk rode back to get the women and bring them to help skin, gut, and butcher the two animals. It would take most of the day to complete the butchering and another storm was coming, but they managed to get it done, and before long there was fresh meat hanging in the smokehouse, enough to last a month or more.

As winter turned into spring, Lazarus planned to get some trapping done. It was now the middle of March, and Lazarus and Hawk Eyes and their families traveled to the Bitterroot River to find prime beaver hunting grounds. They had to be careful, since grizzly bears were now coming out of hibernation and they were known to forage near river beds. Especially mothers with cubs.

Both Angus White Cloud and Amos Winter Hawk were growing fast and were now riding in front of their mothers on horses as they traveled with their parents. The Bitterroot River flowed northward at the confluence of Clark Fork River, through the Bitterroot Valley. It was deep in Flathead country and was not only teeming with beavers, but plenty of fish as well. Lazarus planned to spend most of the spring season trapping up and down the river. He had suggested to his family and in-laws that they go and visit the Nez Perce at the end of the season. This pleased not only both Mountain Flower and Hawk Eyes, but even Plain Feather and Dark Wind, who had friends among the Nez Perce and would be glad to see them again. Dark Wind's family had never been to the village of Stone Heart and when they were asked if they would like to go, they were just as excited as their daughter, so the answer was a joyful yes.

As the spring trapping season was going on, Lazarus and his group were bringing in plenty of beaver. By the time the season was over, they had trapped over five hundred plews. A great haul for the season. Around the middle of May, they traveled from the Bitterroot Valley towards Lolo Pass. It had been over a year since they had been to Stone Heart's village, so there was lots of catching up to do. They arrived there about the beginning of the following week and Chief Stone Heart and his people were overjoyed to be reunited with Mountain Flower, Hawk Eyes, and their families. A feast was held for their return and stories were told about what had happened over the past year. Chief Stone Heart and Hawk Eyes' mother Burnt Willow were introduced to Dark Wind's family. Plenty Hawk and Chief Stone Heart embraced each other, while Burnt Willow and Chief Stone Heart's wife Flying Bird welcomed Fighting Bear Woman and Black Butterfly with open arms. Lone Falcon was greeted by both Chief Stone Heart and Hawk Eyes' brothers and sisters as well. It was a great family reunion and it was great to be home.

"It is good to have you among us again, White Bear," said Chief

Stone Heart. "Word of your medicine and that of your wives is growing."

"Oh?" said Lazarus. "How so?"

"I have heard that the Blackfeet paid you and your family a visit last winter," answered Chief Stone Heart. "I heard that with help from the Flathead, you chased them off and now they fear your medicine."

"I give the Blackfeet better credit than that," said Lazarus. "As long as I stay away from their land, then hopefully they stay away from mine."

"The Blackfeet were not the only problems we had last winter, Uncle," said Mountain Flower.

"Oh?"

Mountain Flower told about how Lazarus helped the Crow repel the Lakota last winter, killing a Lakota warrior in the process. She told of that warrior's sister Soaring Eagle Woman, a woman warrior of her tribe, who wanted revenge on Lazarus. He tried to make peace with her on numerous occasions, but she wouldn't hear of it. She spoke of the Battle at the Belle Fourche River and how she, Dark Wind, Plain Feather, Hawk Eyes, Lone Falcon, and a war party of both Flathead and Crow defeated the Lakota.

Chief Stone Heart and those on the council were impressed. But that wasn't the entire story. "What your niece fails to mention is how she, Dark Wind, and Plain Feather saved my life by killing Soaring Eagle Woman," said Lazarus. "I would not be here to tell you about it if it wasn't for them."

Everyone looked at the wives and aunt of White Bear with new respect.

"This is good," said Chief Stone Heart. "But I am curious, White Bear, why did you attempt to make peace with this woman warrior who sought to kill you?"

"I did and it was refused, several time. And because I don't believe in striking down a woman or making war on them, the fight was inevitable," answered Lazarus. "That is not who I am, to needlessly kill a woman."

"Our husband is an honorable man, who will fight to defend those he loves," said Dark Wind. "And we will fight to defend him from anyone who threatens his life as well."

"The Creator has blessed you indeed, White Bear," said Chief Stone Heart.

"In more ways than one," responded Lazarus. "For that I am truly grateful."

18

OLD FRIENDS AND GOOD NEWS

LAZARUS and his family stayed among the Nez Perce until the end of May. During that time, Lazarus managed to search for new beaver hunting grounds in order for him to trap in the future. He felt that he had enough plews to trade for supplies for the next two seasons. In the first week of June, Lazarus and his family left the village of Stone Heart and headed back east. Their goal was to head to Fort Lisa and trade in their plews from the last two seasons. They were going to stop at their home in Silver Bow Valley to retrieve their cache of plews from last winter season, before heading to the Crow village of Chief Medicine Hawk.

"I can't wait to return home to my people," said Plain Feather. "I have wonderful news to tell them."

"What news would that be?" asked Lazarus.

"Hawk Eyes is going to be a father!"

Hawk Eyes' eyes became wide as saucers. "Are you sure?" he asked.

"I am sure," answered Plain Feather. "Little White Cloud is going to have a playmate next winter."

Hawk Eyes hugged his wife, before both he and Lazarus screamed out a WAUGH! Lazarus was excited because he was going to have another cousin. Even though he was not related to Hawk Eyes by any means, he still considered him family.

Mountain Flower was happy for Plain Feather and Hawk Eyes, but she felt a little emptiness. She had been married to Lazarus for three years now and she had not gotten pregnant. She wanted to have his baby and it bothered her that she couldn't. Not as much as it used to, though, because Lazarus never treated her differently than Dark Wind. He loved both of his wives affectionately and equally and always encouraged Mountain Flower to have faith and be patient. Dark Wind was the same way. She prayed that the Creator would bless Mountain Flower with a child of her own as well, so little Winter Hawk could have a brother or sister to play with. The two wives of the man known as White Bear had grown to become like sisters and they loved and treated each other as such. Lazarus always found it amazing that there was no jealousy between his wives and was grateful for it.

After they arrived home in the Silver Bow Valley, they stayed for a few days. Lazarus and Hawk Eyes would dig up their cache of over three hundred beaver plews from last winter to add to their five hundred and fifty from this past spring. Plenty Hawk, Fighting Bear Woman, Lone Falcon, and Black Butterfly went to visit their people in Chief Snake Killer's village. However, they returned a few days later because they wanted to accompany Lazarus and his family east to Fort Lisa. They had never been that far east in Omaha country, but they knew that they would have to pass enemy territory, such as the Cheyenne, Arapaho, and Lakota. Both Lazarus and Hawk Eyes not only welcomed their company, but thought that having the extra bodies them with them would be sound as they traveled through enemy country. Safety in numbers.

By the second week of June, they left Silver Bow Valley with their pack animals carrying their plews and travois carrying their lodges. They traveled from the Clark Fork River heading south. They wanted to avoid Three Forks, which was in Blackfoot Country, so they crossed the Big Hole River to the Red Rock River into Yellowstone country, where Yellowstone National Park now stands. They hunted along the way, capturing mostly mule deer and bighorn sheep. They avoided grizzly bears that had been out and about since spring, but they did manage to shoot at least two black bears. The added bear grease was a welcomed commodity as well as the meat. The women would dig up edible plant roots to add to their diet and they stayed no more than a week in Yellowstone country to work on the two bear skins, before continuing their travels. Buffalo was plentiful, as well, but both Lazarus and his wives suggested that hunting the shaggy beast could wait until after they reached the eastern plains.

By the middle of the month, they found the Crow village of Chief Medicine Hawk, near the Little Bighorn River. As they stayed with them, Plain Feather informed her parents that they were going to have another grandchild. Medicine Hawk and Blue Willow were overjoyed. They loved being grandparents and enjoyed playing with not just Angus White Cloud, but Amos Winter Hawk, too. Upon seeing Lone Falcon and Black Butterfly's baby boy Panther, Blue Willow's heart melted. She held Panther in her arms, while Angus White Cloud and Amos Winter Hawk sat on Medicine Hawk's lap. The smiles on all the grandparents' faces were priceless.

"This is what we live for every day," said Chief Medicine Hawk. "These are our future."

"Indeed," responded Plenty Hawk.

For Lazarus, Dark Wind and Mountain Flower, they couldn't have been happier. While they sojourned in the Silver Bow Valley, they also considered the village of Chief Medicine Hawk their home as well. Lazarus always considered the Crow Chief and his wife family since their eldest daughter was married to his late uncle. Nothing would ever change that. Amos Winter Hawk hopped off Medicine Hawk's lap and slowly walked to his father, holding out his arms. Without hesitation, Lazarus picked up his only son and bounced him on his knee. The little two-year-old could pass for a full-blooded Flathead Indian, but his hair had become silvery gray and his eyes were blue. He also had his father's nose, but his mother's cheeks. As Lazarus Buchanan tickled his son, thoughts of his kin back east appeared unbidden.

As if reading their husband's mind, both Dark Wind and Mountain Flower, who were sitting next to him, got his attention.

"You still think about your family," said Dark Wind. "Don't you?"

"You are my family," answered Lazarus. "My place is here with all of you."

"I would still love to meet the people that Dark Wind and I owe our happiness to," said Mountain Flower. "Especially your grandfather, who both you and your uncle spoke fondly of."

Lazarus sighed. "I'm not sure my grandfather is still alive," he said. "It has been over five summers since I left Delaware." *Had it really been that long already?* he thought to himself.

"You rarely speak of your family back where you come from," said Chief Medicine Hawk.

"A thing I myself have noticed," added Lone Falcon.

Lazarus just shrugged. He talked about his family, the place he was born, where his parents and grandfather came from and why he begged his Uncle Amos to bring him out west to become a trapper. Everyone listened and soaked up the information as Lazarus told them about his family. While he would never admit it, deep down he missed his family, and his wives, in-laws, and friends could sense it.

"We should visit your family, nephew," said Plain Feather. "I believe your Uncle would have wanted us to meet them and see how your people live."

"I don't know if that is a good idea," said Lazarus. "My uncle didn't trust most of our kind, especially our family. Besides, the only member of my family that he was closest to, besides me, was my grandfather."

"Be that as it may," said Mountain Flower, "I still say that we should visit your people."

"I agree," added Dark Wind. "It would be good for the children to see some part of their father's world."

"I myself have been interested in where you white men come from and how you live," said Plenty Hawk.

"I fear all of you will be disappointed," said Lazarus. "Where I come from is not like out here. I would be afraid for all of you."

"You're afraid how your people would treat us," said Hawk Eyes. That was a statement, not a question.

Lazarus nodded. "At least here, I know where I stand," he said. "I know who I can trust and I can protect my loved ones better, but back where I come from, that is something else."

Both Dark Wind and Mountain Flower gently placed a hand on their husband's. They knew he had their best interests at heart and they weren't alone.

"A wise man told me once," said Plain Feather, "that a person will never know how to live, if they let fear dictate the way they live."

"Who was this wise man?" asked Lazarus.

"He was your Uncle."

The trapper just smiled as he put his arms around his wives. Little Amos Winter Hawk was getting sleepy, so he just laid his head on his father's chest.

"Maybe someday we will go and visit my people," said Lazarus. "If God wills it."

"I would like that," said Dark Wind.

"As would I," added Mountain Flower.

They stayed with the Crow until the end of June. Lazarus and his family then left the village of Chief Medicine Hawk and headed east, traveling through the Powder River country, crossing the Little Missouri River to the Belle Fourche River. They followed the Belle Fourche River to the Cheyenne River before heading south to the White River, following it to the Missouri River. Despite traveling through both Cheyenne and Lakota territories, the group managed to avoid any encounters with roving war and hunting parties from the two tribes. While they followed the Missouri River south, they managed to hunt buffalo, taking down two adult cows from a herd near the Keya Paha River. They stayed there for a couple of days, before continuing south. They arrived at Fort Lisa, which was in Omaha country, around the middle of July.

Fort Lisa was built in 1812 in what is now North Omaha, Nebraska. It was named after the co-owner and founder of the Missouri Fur Company, Manuel Lisa, who Lazarus Buchanan and his late uncle

Amos MacKinnon met, but instead of trading their plews with him, they often went straight to St. Louis and traded with Lisa's partners. However, with both his uncle and his friend John Colter now dead, Lazarus no longer saw any reason to travel to St. Louis. With the amount of plews he and Hawk Eyes trapped these past two seasons, he felt that they could get a fair deal in supplies from Manuel Lisa at his fort.

As Lazarus and his group traveled to the fort, bypassing an Omaha village, a group of Omaha warriors approached them. The leader of the group recognized Lazarus and gave a smile, as he and his men stopped in front of them.

"It is good to see you again, White Bear," he signed.

At first Lazarus didn't recognize the man, then suddenly it hit him.

"Raven?" he shouted.

The man nodded. Both men dismounted and greeted each other with a hug. They had not seen each other in over a year. Raven remembered Lazarus' wives and they remembered him and after they dismounted, he greeted them with hugs as well.

"It is good to see you again, Raven," said Dark Wind. "How is Red Bird?"

"She is well," answered Raven. "She and my brother will be happy to see you."

"And how is your daughter?" asked Lazarus. "In good health I pray."

"She is well," answered Raven. "Growing and becoming more beautiful, like her mother."

Lazarus and his wives introduced Raven to Plain Feather, Hawk Eyes, and Dark Wind's family. The Omaha warrior greeted Plenty Hawk, Lone Falcon, and their wives with the peace sign.

"I welcome you among my people," he signed. "Any friend of White Bear is a friend of mine."

"We are honored to be here," signed Plenty Hawk. "White Bear is truly a good friend to have."

"I agree," said Raven. "Especially since his medicine has grown over the past year."

"What do you mean?" asked Lazarus.

"About a moon ago," answered Raven. "Some Oglala Lakota came to the fort to trade. They spoke about how a warrior woman among their people was killed in battle last winter, by a white trapper with white hair."

"Was her name Soaring Eagle Woman?"

"Matter of fact her name was Soaring Eagle Woman," answered Raven.

"Not all of that story is true," said Lazarus.

"Which part?"

"I didn't kill her," answered Lazarus. "My wives and my uncle's widow did."

"Really?" said Raven. He looked at Dark Wind, Mountain Flower, and Plain Feather, who acknowledged that they killed the Oglala Lakota Warrior woman when she tried to kill Lazarus. Raven nodded his approval and his respect for the three women increased.

"You should tell us this tonight at the feast," said Raven.

"I don't know about that, my friend," said Lazarus.

At first Raven was confused, but he didn't push the issue. He sensed that there was more to the story and neither Lazarus nor his family cared to talk about it.

"Will you at least come visit our village?"

"Of course we will," answered Lazarus. "But first, we must go to the fort to trade."

Raven nodded before remounting his horse as he and his warriors bade their leave. It was clear to Lazarus that they were a hunting party, not a war party, so they knew there was definitely going to be a feast tonight.

They entered the fort and stood in line. Manuel Lisa, who had open trade with the Omaha tribe last year was standing not far from one of the trading tents inside the post. The forty-two-year-old Spaniard saw Lazarus and his family from a distance and recognized them. He went to greet them without hesitation.

"Welcome, Senor Buchanan," he said.

"Hello, Senor Lisa," responded Lazarus. "How's business?"

"*Muy bueno*," answered Manuel Lisa. "Now that the war with the British is finally over."

"It is?" asked a surprised Lazarus. "When did this happen?"

"Back in February," answered Manuel Lisa. "General Andrew Jackson defeated the British at the Battle of New Orleans back in January, forcing the British to sue for peace, so in February they ratified the Treaty of Ghent."

"Thank God," said Lazarus. "That means the Fur Trade can resume without problems."

"They'll always be problems, *mi amigo*," said Manuel Lisa. "Otherwise, how else will you have competition?"

"True," said Lazarus.

Manuel Lisa looked at Lazarus' pack laden animals and was impressed. "It appears that you and yours have done well over the past seasons," he said.

"Aye," responded Lazarus.

"I assume you're here to trade?"

Lazarus nodded.

"Well then, I assure you that you will be given a good price."

"Thank you, Senor Lisa," said Lazarus.

The Spaniard doffed his hat and bowed before Lazarus and his family. Lazarus didn't fully like or trust Manuel Lisa and he wasn't the only one. Manuel Lisa may have been a cagey businessman, but he was not very well liked, even among trappers. His quick temper was legendary and how he conducted business with those who worked for him was very controversial. However, Lazarus was a free trapper and he believed that Manuel Lisa was a man of his word. If he said that he would offer a fair price, then he likely would.

Lazarus and Hawk Eyes got $8 a pound for their 850 plews. While that was less than what they would have gotten in St. Louis, it was still a lot of money. They resupplied themselves for the next two seasons and bought foofaraw for their wives and family and friends back west. After all the shopping was done, they kept their promise to visit Raven and his brother Chief Yellow Bull that evening.

Yellow Bull was the man who gave Lazarus his Indian name, White Bear. Like Raven, he heard about the trapper's increased reputation against the Lakota last winter. While Lazarus didn't care to talk about what happened with Soaring Eagle Woman and her people last winter, he did clarify to Yellow Bull that he was not the one who killed her in battle, but it was his wives and his uncle's widow. Yellow Bull accepted that and held a feast both for Lazarus and his family's honor.

It was good to be among old friends again and as the feast was held, Lazarus again thought about how far he had come over the past five years.

Damn, he thought to himself. *I can't believe it has been five years already.*

While his family and friends feasted on buffalo and other meat, Lazarus looked up in the sky for a minute, before turning his attention back to his wives, aunt Plain Feather, Hawk Eyes, and his son and cousin. "I really miss Uncle Amos," he said to himself. "I hope I made you proud."

EPILOGUE

MEANWHILE IN DOVER, Delaware, seventy-year old Angus MacKinnon was sitting in his rocking chair. It had been a year since he survived a near fatal heart attack, and he was forced to turn over his boxing school to one of his pupils. Since then, he had enjoyed some of the comforts that life had to offer. His great-grandson Paul Buchanan Jr. would be five in a few months and had become the apple of his eye. The little tyke inherited the white hair of his great-grandfather, which was rare, since neither Angus' daughter, Lydia Buchanan, her husband Peter Buchanan, or their two eldest sons Peter Jr. and Paul Sr. had white hair. If anything, the only descendants of the aging Scotsman that inherited his white hair were his son Amos and his youngest grandson Lazarus and his only granddaughter Leah.

Amos and Lazarus.

A sense of sadness showed on Angus' face as memories of his only son and his youngest grandson came to his mind. He couldn't believe it had been over five years since Amos came home to visit from the frontier and Lazarus begged him to take him when he returned the frontier. Angus remembered how upset his daughter and son-in-law were. However, he knew that Lazarus was not happy living at home with his parents. He wanted adventure, just like his uncle, and his uncle Amos was more than happy to oblige him.

Now Angus wondered what had become of his only son and youngest grandson. Were they still alive? He prayed for it to be so. So lost in his thoughts was he that he didn't hear his son-in-law walk up behind him.

"You okay, Angus?" asked Peter Buchanan Sr.

"I'm fine. Just thinking."

"About what?"

"Our sons. Yours and mine."

"You mean Amos and Lazarus." That was a statement not a question. "I miss them, too. Especially Lazarus."

"How old would he be now?"

"Twenty-one."

Angus just sighed. "He is a man now," he said.

"If he and Amos are still alive," said Peter.

"I hope they still are," said Angus. "For Lydia's sake."

Peter nodded his head in agreement. "I hope wherever they are, they are at least happy and have found some peace."

For the first time, his father-in-law smiled.

"Aye," he said. "Me, too."

AUTHOR'S NOTE

Contrary to popular belief, warrior women among the plains tribes were not rare. Up until recently, their stories had been written out of American history. Some of the most famous warrior women in American history were just as fierce, brave, and courageous as their male counterparts. Some of the best known warrior women were Pine Leaf (of the Gros Ventre, but captured and adopted by the Crow); Buffalo Calf Road Woman (Cheyenne), who fought at the Battle of The Little Bighorn and may have dealt the fatal blow that ended the life of George Custer; Pretty Nose (Arapaho), who also fought at the Battle of The Little Bighorn, was a Chief, and lived to be 101 years old; Lozen (Chiricahua Apache), who fought alongside Geronimo; Dahteste (Mescalero Apache), who also rode with Geronimo and acted as a translator for her people and was designated to lead in treaty negotiations with American and Mexican armies; Running Eagle (Piegan Blackfeet); and Osh-Tich (Crow) who fought against the Lakota and Cheyenne at the Battle of The Rosebud.

The list goes on and on. As a history major with a minor in Native American Studies, I am happy to say that the stories of warrior women from American history are finally being told and honored in a respectful way. While this book, like all my books, is a work of fiction, I was inspired by what I learned at Montana State University about women warriors and from other historical fiction novels that had women warriors in them. I hope you all enjoy reading this third book in *The Frontier* series as much as I did writing it.

ABOUT THE AUTHOR

LeRoy A. Peters is an Air Force veteran and graduate of Montana State University in Bozeman, MT.

He is a published author of the Edge Of The World Trilogy and Saga Of The Armstrong Brothers series and has published a standalone novel entitled Where The Wind Takes You. He is a huge fan of authors who have written novels set in the Fur Trade, such as the late Win Blevins, the late Richard S. Wheeler, Lane R. Warenski, David Robbins, D.L. Bittick, Porter Mills III, John Legg, M. Wayne Zillman, Robert M. Johnson, W. Michael Gear, and the late Terry C. Johnstone. He is a strong advocate for American Indian rights and has read books of famous American Indian heroes such as Sitting Bull, Gall, Crazy Horse, Geronimo, Black Kettle, Logan Fontenelle, Quanah Parker and in recent times Dennis Banks. A native of Clarksville, Maryland, he currently resides in Newark, Delaware.

Made in the USA
Columbia, SC
24 August 2024

41115518R00061